Will you still love me tomorrow? 2

Ebony Diamonds

Contents

Donathon

"**Y**ou know I wouldn't miss this for the world. I'm so proud of you, baby," I kissed her, and before we pulled off, I wanted to pop the question.

"I have something I need to ask you."

She started to look nervous, and I eased her a little when I pulled out the ring. She put her hand over her mouth in shock. Before I could ask, she screamed.

"Yes, of course I will."

I might have been worried about the bank shit, but she'd just made me the happiest man in the world.

"I love you, Tori." I pulled her face to mine and kissed her deeply.

"I love you too, Donathon. Now let's go before we're late, future husband."

I was all smiles driving to the campus. We got inside and she ran off to be with her class. I sat right behind them and immediately put on a scowl. I saw Rita and Celine sitting on my right. Rita waved and smiled at me. I just looked forward. As the graduation progressed, I watched my baby cross the stage, and she blew a kiss at me. I looked at Rita, and she had a death stare on her face.

"Before we end the commencement, we have a video from the graduating class."

The video played, and as I was watching the students say their majors and plans for the future, I saw Rita and Celine get up and walk to the front. Everybody watched them go to the stage. For some reason, Celine ran off, but I saw Larrise standing up front looking dazed. Rita called out for Celine, but she kept running.

"I have something to say. One of your senior class students is a known prostitute in the area, and she shouldn't be sitting here all high and mighty," Rita said into the microphone.

What the fuck was she up to now?

"Young lady, what do you think you're doing?" One of the men onstage came up and tried to move her from the mic.

"I'm speaking truths today." I could see Tori looking red, and she had tears forming in her eyes when she looked back at me.

What the hell was going on here? Larrise limped up on stage and grabbed the microphone.

"Yes, she is speaking the truth. Tori Minors is a whore, and she sells her pussy to anybody with a dollar in their pocket. She and I would go to Lacey's and fuck a bunch of men we didn't know. I bet she didn't tell y'all she had an abortion because she was pregnant with professor Marlow's baby."

She started sticking her tongue out and doing some crack head ass dance while pointing at Tori. Everybody gasped, and I saw a guy get up and walk out. He must have been the guy they were talking about. This couldn't be right; Tori isn't that kind of person. I couldn't believe Larrise, but I could definitely believe

Rita would be up to some shit like this.

I saw Tori start talking on the screen. She was saying her major, and then the screen blanked out. The next thing I saw was a video of Tori and Jaden fucking. I had to be tripping because I know they wouldn't do this shit to me. My world crumbled right before my eyes. I saw Tori get up and run to the stage, and she started to beat the shit out of Rita. Larrise ran off and made a quick exit out the door before Tori could get to her. She fucked my best friend? How could she do this to me? I got up completely embarrassed, and left. I heard Tori calling behind me and I kept walking, I couldn't face her.

"Don, please let me explain." I stopped and turned around.

"Explain what? You fucked my best friend and accepted a ring from me? What was she talking about? You're a prostitute, Tori?"

She looked away. "I was escorting before I ran back into you. I needed to pay tuition and bills. I just didn't know any other way. The thing with Jaden was he made me, baby. You gotta believe that," she said, crying uncontrollably.

"Are you fucking serious? I've been kissing you and sticking my dick in a fucking hoe? I wanted marry you, but I can't turn a hoe into a house wife. I'm out of here. By the way, Whori, nobody can make you meet them and fuck them." I was so disgusted.

I saw the pain those words caused, but I couldn't deal with this right now.

"Don, please don't leave me again. I can't handle it again."

I just shook my head and turned my back on her. She ran out the building, and I wasn't even going to follow. I was done with her. How could she keep this from me? And she fucked Jaden at that. I was walking to my car when I heard a woman scream and what sounded like a car accident.

"Oh my God. She just jumped in front of my car. I saw her. She did it on purpose," I heard a woman scream.

I ran over in time to see the blood seeping from Tori's mouth.

"Tori! please don't die!"

I grabbed my phone as I kneeled beside her and called 911. She tried to kill herself because of me. I felt like shit, but I still wasn't ready to forgive her, and I don't know if I ever would be.

Tori

"Tori, you can't just lay here. If you don't get up, you won't get better." My mother tried to get me up out of my hospital bed for therapy.

For months, I lay there, not wanting to do anything. I hadn't seen Donathan since the last night I was in the hospital, before they transferred me here. The nurses finally told me that every night he came in there and would leave in the morning before I woke up. The last night, I stayed up, and just when I was falling asleep he came in. He was about to turn and leave before I stopped him.

"Please don't leave," I said with my good arm held up, reaching for him.

"I can't even face you, Tori. It's easy when you're asleep because I can tell you how I feel, but I can't look you in the eye and know you did that shit," he said, standing by the door.

"I didn't have a choice. I had no money, I had nothing. I was going to have to drop out of school," I pleaded and cried. It hurt to even do that.

"You had choices. And Jaden?" he asked.

"He was blackmailing me. I did it for you. He was hurting me, bad," I cried, feeling sick from even thinking about it.

"I don't know what you want me to do, Tori. I should just forget it?"

he asked, shaking his head.

"I love you," I pleaded.

"I love you too, more than anything. I just can't be with you, Tori, not right now," he said and left the room.

His last words never left me. I was in a deep depression, and I didn't know how to get out of it. He left me again. When I needed him, he left. I was done with his chapter in my life. We obviously weren't meant to be.

I was in a private facility that my mother chose. I had a room that looked like a five-star hotel, and it cost a lot of money. She had somehow come up on a fortune. I had called my lawyers and banks to make sure she hadn't stolen from me. She didn't, so I didn't know where she had gotten that money from.

"Hey, K.C.," my mother gushed. K.C had been coming since I was moved here. I didn't really want company, nor did I want any-body to see me looking like this.

"How you doing Ms. Minors?" he said and hugged her. She'd had a little crush on him since she met him. "Boo, you feeling bet-ter today?" he asked, coming around to sit next to me.

"I'm fine," I said, looking forward.

"I brought you some Now and Laters. I know you like them," he said as he setting the pack on the table.

"I'm about to go. See if you can get her to go to therapy, please," my mother said before grabbing her purse and leaving.

"I wished I could put her on a block list for the hospital," I said, smiling a little at K.C.

He laughed at my comment. "I miss you, Tori. Let's get you better so we can chill like we used to, boo," he said, rubbing my leg.

I was glad that after the surgeries it was feeling better. I couldn't hide the fact that I still loved how he called me boo, but that shit only triggered painful emotions.

"I was so stupid, K.C.," I said, crying and covering my face.

"You just had to do some shit you didn't want to do to get by. Man, we all do shit we have to do sometimes." He pulled the cover off my face and wiped my tears with his hand.

"Thank you," I said, sniffling.

He took some tissue out the box and gave it to me. "No thanks needed. I care a lot about you, girl. I know I fucked up that one time when I said that slick shit to you, but you knew me better than that. A lot changed since you been in here, so I want you to come stay at my house until you 100, aight? I got a therapist ready to help you and all," he said, swiping his hand across the air to emphasize the point.

"You don't have to do all that for no hoe, K.C.," I said and looked past him.

"Tori, stop saying that shit! You a beautiful ass queen." He smiled. I felt like crying, though. He kicked off his shoes and closed the door, then got into the bed with me and held me tightly. "Take a nap," he ordered while stroking the side of my head.

It was only after four, but since I always felt beat down, I drifted off easily.

When I woke up, K.C was snoring in the back of my head like a damn grizzly. I didn't want to disturb him, so I tried to get up to go the bathroom.

He quickly jumped up. "What you need, boo?" he said, climbing out the bed to help me.

"I was just going to the bathroom, boy." I laughed and looked outside. It was dark, and all the lights were shining. Damn, we must have been asleep for a while.

"Well, I can help you to the bathroom."

"K.C.! You don't have to baby me!" I yelled at him.

"Look I'm just tryna help, you don't have to act like a bitch," he said as he put on his shoes.

He was probably right, I was acting like a bitch. I shouldn't take my frustrations out on him. I limped over to where he was tying his shoe. He stood up and looked over my head.

"I'm sorry." I wrapped my non slinged arm around him.

He was reluctant at first, but he wrapped his arms around me as well.

"I know you not feeling this shit in here, but if you want to, I can get you out of here right now so you can be comfortable," he said, grabbing my hand, and kissing it.

"How can you be so cool about this? You know what I did with these men?" I cried. I didn't understand how he could see a queen in me.

"Tori, you're STD free, and I'm sure you brushed your teeth. You're still a person, that don't mean you don't deserve the best. I know you don't like me like that, but I still consider you my friend."

"I always liked you, I just didn't think you would go for some normal girl like me," I said with a grin.

"Damn, and I thought I was pressing up on you the whole time," he said with a serious ass sexy look on his face.

"Can you really get me out of here?" I asked. I was ready to get out of hospitals period.

"Yeah, I got a therapy room in my house, you can stay however long you want. I won't be there to bother you," K.C. said as he grabbed up my things.

"You know I got my own house, right?" I asked as I walked into the bathroom.

"Yeah, but do you have a state of the art gym? You can use it like a rehab center. I won't be there much anyway, plus I'ma be leaving for a few months, so it's all you. I already got therapist ready for you."

"How the hell can you afford all of that? Did I miss something?" I yelled through the door. I just realized he said he had a new house. When I came out, he was holding up a Hawks Jersey with his last name.

"I told you, you missed some shit. I got drafted to the Hawks, shawty." He put his hands up.

"Oh, my God, congratulations K.C., or do I start calling you Kadeem Coates NBA star?" I said and pushed him.

"Don't be saying my name out here, these broads might recognize me," he joked.

"Well, we can talk about it on the way out. I'm ready to get out of here," I said as I put on K.C.'s jacket.

"Don't you got to sign out? You can barely walk without help. Don't you need a wheel chair?" he asked, looking around the room.

"You ain't a big man no more?" I teased.

He picked me up and we walked out the room.

"I'm leaving," I told the nurses as we walked by.

"Ms. Minors, you need therapy!" the nurse yelled from behind us.

For some reason, me and K.C just laughed.

Donathon

As each day passed, my house seemed more and more like a prison. I never went anywhere or did anything for months, because I was so fucked up mentally, and I didn't know what my next move was. I didn't even want to be near fucking Texas. I decided to pack my shit up and roll. I had tried to find a way to forgive her and move on, but it was too much. I hoped she wouldn't hate me for not trying harder, but I needed time away from her.

I was ready to marry her, and she was just going to let me, knowing what she was doing. I know I wasn't shit for not telling her about what I do, but damn. I tried not to think about it, so I turned on the TV and started watching the news as I packed.

The police have identified the body of 24-year-old Sabrina Johnson after dental records confirmed this was indeed the mother of two. She was 9 months pregnant, and the police are now looking for her son, whom they hope is still alive.

What the fuck was wrong with people? I turned on basketball, then started packing some more. There was a knock on the door, and I wondered who the hell it could be. I had been kind of paranoid since that detective came and talked to me that time about the robbery.

When I went to the door, I saw that I may have had a reason to feel like this. There was a black Impala out front with the lights on. I didn't even give a fuck right now, I was ready. When I swung the door open, there were two uniformed officers and a woman in a suit.

"Donathan Gray?" the black one asked.

"Yeah." I was about to put my hands behind my head.

"Your wife, Rita Gray, when was the last time you saw her." They both looked at me, awaiting my response.

"Almost a year, why?" I was starting to think something had happened to her. No matter how stupid I think she is, I wouldn't want to see her hurt.

"Well, we need to talk to her regarding Sabrina Johnson. We talked to Ms. Johnson's sister and the last time she was seen, she said she was meeting her therapist, your wife."

"She my ex-wife, first off, and second, I don't know shit about that. I left her ass a year ago, and the last time I saw her was at my girlfriend's graduation. June ninth."

They looked at each other.

"That was the day she went missing," the white one said.

"Thanks for your help, if you hear from her, we need you to let her know she needs to come in."

They both turned and walked down the steps.

I know Rita was cray, but she wouldn't do no shit like that. Either way, I wouldn't be here for the shit because I decided I was leaving tonight. Of course, I needed to say bye to Tori for good, though. I wrote her a letter, but tore it up. This needed to be done face to face, so I was going to see if she was in the rehab center the nurse told me she had been transferred to.

I had asked one of the nurses to keep me updated on how she was doing after the night Tori caught me coming to be with her while she slept. The last time I called, I found out she'd left, and I figured she was good, and at least that made me feel a little better. I had the name of the place, so I put it in my GPS and saw it was only twenty minutes from me. After I loaded all the suit cases that would fit in my truck, I said fuck all the rest of that shit.

This GPS wasn't worth shit as I followed its fucked-up directions the whole ride. I didn't know what I was going to say, so I kept going over it in my head until I felt comfortable. When I got out the car I saw Tori's mother stomping out of the building. Damn, I should have run her ass over.

She saw me and shook her head. "She isn't here, if that's what you're doing here," she said, pushing a cart full of stuff.

"Why the fuck else would I be here?" I asked, stopping the cart.

"She left with K.C., a real man, a successful man who won't leave her in a hospital alone. Just leave her alone, she only seems to be down when you're around, just like when you were teens. Just leave my daughter alone," she said and yanked the cart then walked past me.

"What you even doing' here? You trying to get to her money, huh?" I yelled behind her.

Tori was smart, though, she probably saw through her fake ass caring routine. She got in her car and drove off. I decided to follow her because regardless of what happened, I wanted to see Tori just to say goodbye.

I followed the bitch to Afton Oaks. This was a rich ass neighborhood from what I could see. I saw she pulled into a beige painted house. Whoever owned that place had money. She got out the car and I saw the front door open. That nigga K.C. came out and grabbed some of the stuff from her hand. Then I saw Tori standing in the doorway. She had on a pair of shorts, and I could see one of her legs was wrapped in a bandage. She held a cane in her left hand, but she still looked like a 10.

I got out and jogged up to the curb. "Tori!"

"Don."

"What the hell is your problem?" her mother yelled at me.

I put up my middle finger at her and focused on Tori.

"Bruh, the fuck you poppin' up at my shit for?" K.C. said like he wanted a problem.

He was a big nigga, but we would go blow for blow if he ain't fall the fuck back.

"I came to talk to Tori, nigga. You ain't got to be hard cuz she right there, baby boy."

"Stop, both of y'all," Tori yelled, limping down the steps.

"Tori, you shouldn't be—"

"I can handle myself, Ma," she snapped at her mother.

I walked up, and she stepped back.

"I just wanted to say bye, and to tell you that I love you, baby, and ain't shit you done gonna change that," I said and kissed her on the cheek.

"So, that's just it? Everything is just over? Your love wasn't deeper than a puddle, nigga," she said, then turned around and walked back toward the house.

As selfish as the shit sounded, I wanted her to tell me she loved me too. K.C helped her in the house, and Tori's mother smirked and got back into her car. I kept thinking I should put her out her misery, but instead, I got in my car and left. I got on the highway and headed toward DC, not even looking back.

Rita

The mobile lightly played the tune of "Rock a Bye Baby," while rocking Alexandro to sleep. He really needed to take his nap; he was so fussy when he didn't want to go to sleep. I called him Ali for short. He was getting so big and was turning one in a few months. I couldn't wait to throw his party. I was now living in Atlanta and had started completely over. My family had been calling me over and over, leaving voicemails telling me the police were looking for me.

I had changed my name to Ellie Santia and hired a full-time nanny when I first left Houston because I had full facial restructuring. I didn't look anything like myself, and that's exactly what I wanted. New Social security number and birthday, it was so legit, I got a driver's license. I was a new bitch all together.

I met the local university's Senior Vice president at a party. He was so handsome for an older man, and he didn't resist me for a minute. I fucked him stupid, and he pulled some strings. I now have a Bachelor's degree in pre-law under my alias, and after sucking his dick like a champ, he agreed to hook me up with his buddy who was the president of the law school. I got close to him too, real close. He wasn't as easy as I thought, but after our last sexual encounter, I pretty much could blackmail him into letting me graduate from law school without a day in class. He thought I would tell his wife and his colleagues that he liked to get fucked in the ass with a dildo, so my wish is his command

I wanted to move back to Texas, and I wanted to make sure I could get a job. There were too many hoops for me to try and get a new license illegally.

Ali finally lay down, and I started to clean up a little. I had a nice little house in Cobb county that I had rented from this older woman I met in the grocery store. She was gushing over Ali, and I asked if she knew of any nice apartment communities I could check out. I had just moved here, and we were staying in a hotel. She told me her husband had just died, and she couldn't bear to stay in the house any longer. I moved right in. I loved it too, but I wanted to be closer to my husband. I couldn't wait to introduce him to our son.

I had a plan that was foolproof. I was going to get him to fall in love with Ellie, and we would get married again and live happily ever after. We would have our baby, and everything would be perfect again.

While Ali slept, I went online and searched some rentals in Houston. I was still living off money from my ex, son of a bitch, so I could afford to still live as good as I have been before.

The next day, I got a U-Haul and hired some movers to pack it up. I paid them to drive the truck to Texas. I had a few job interviews setup, so I planned to stop and get the keys to my new house, and grab some interview clothes. I had to check out a few daycare centers because I refused to put my son in anything less than five stars.

Once Ali was loaded into the car, I hit the road. The drive wasn't that long, so I planned to drive straight there except stopping for food and change to Ali. Two hours into the drive, I heard the news station report to be on the lookout for Rita Gray. My heart started beating fast, but I wasn't worried because I was no longer her.

I continued driving until I got to a rest area, then I called my friend, Marlina. She was the only person who knew who I was now. I knew she wouldn't say anything because of what I had done for her. Her husband was beating her and we killed him then buried his body at a construction site. She owed me everything. She had gotten a nice ass check from his death once they found all the blood we let spill in his truck. They knew nobody could survive losing that amount of blood.

"Hola, mami," I said into the phone.

"Que pasa perra."

"I'm almost there, I wanted to know if you heard the radio?" I asked.

"Sure did, that bitch crazy, huh?" she said, speaking in code.

"Yup, so look, I'm almost there, just wanted to check in."

I was pretty much letting her know if the police came not to say shit. I hung up and finished feeding Ali, and we got back on the road. Before we pulled off, I went on my new Facebook page and saw he had accepted my friend request.

I smirked. I have a second chance with my man.

*****

Three weeks later, I felt settled into our new home. Ali's bedroom was beautifully setup with blue paint and shelves of toys. I had gone to Ikea and got his room together. He had a new bed and everything. I loved being a mother, and I always knew I would make a good one. No matter how I got him, he was mine. I'm sure I rescued him from hell, and now his life was going to be perfect.

I was just dropping him off at day care. I liked the place, and I felt like they were genuine, not like the fake ones who were nice when you're there and treat your kids like shit when you're not. I had an interview with Coates and Associates. I was scared shitless too. I had fake results for passing the bar with a fake license to go with it.

When I pulled into the garage of the building, I consulted the mirror and made sure my makeup and hair was nice, then I got out and grabbed the new Samsonite briefcase I picked up yesterday. I pressed the elevator and waited for the car to arrive.

I heard footsteps, but I smelled cologne before a figure stood next to me. I looked over, and an immediate smile came across my face when the sexy ass dude smiled down at me.

"Good morning," he said in a deep baritone voice.

"Hi." I giggled like a school girl.

We remained quiet when the car came. He motioned for me to go on first, and when I walked past him, I could feel his eyes on my ass.

I noticed he didn't hit a button, which meant he was going to the same floor. We smiled back and forth at each other until we got to the 8th floor.

The door opened, and there were people everywhere. I guess it was starting time for them.

"I guess I will see you around here, huh?" he said as he walked off down the hall.

"Fine, ain't he?" the white girl at the reception desk said.

"I hadn't noticed," I lied.

"Yeah, sure. How can I help you?" She smiled.

"I have an interview today," I told her.

"Okay, sign in, and I will see if your name is on one of the partners' list." She put a pen on the upper counter and went on her computer. I signed my name Ellie Santia on the line of the visitor's log.

"Mr. Coates is ready for you," she said and pointed down the hall.

I walked down the hall looking at all the doors until I reached Anderson Coates.

"I can hear you. Come in," the voice behind the door said.

I walked in and smiled because it was the guy from the elevator.

"Small world, huh?" He smiled back.

"I guess so." I looked around his office and to say I was impressed was an understatement. I could tell by his office that he like nice things.

"So, let's get it started." He sat back behind his desk. "I see you graduated from Clark Atlanta."

He started to run down my education and accomplishments that I'd falsely put on a resume. He went on to explain that with my limited experience, he wasn't sure about hiring me.

"You never had a case before, so the best I can do with you is start you off with civil suits or something. I just have to call your references and—"

I started coughing after sipping on my water to create a distraction. I don't know why I thought I could do this; of course, they check shit. I needed to think of something quick.

"Are you okay?" He rushed over and snatched some napkins out the gold holder.

"I'm fine," I said, patting my chest.

I saw him looking, and I knew it was my chance. I pretended to slip, and fell into his chest.

"Wooohhh, are you okay?" he asked, grabbing me and sitting me down.

He took more napkins and patted the water on my lap. I was smiling, and he must have caught himself.

"Oh, I'm sorry." He shook his head.

I moved my left leg over, and spread my legs a little. I saw him lick his lips, and he looked at my inner thighs. I could see in his eyes that he was wondering what the meeting place between looks like.

"Are you good now?" he asked, leaning back on his desk again.

"Yes, I'm feeling good," I said seductively. "So, what we're saying?" I asked, crossing my leg over.

"When can you start?" he asked with his arms folded.

"Right now," I said, falling to my knees and trying to work on his belt.

"What the… Fuck…" He was cut off by my mouth gripping his dick.

He had a nice ass piece, too. I bobbed my head back and forth. When I looked up, he had the sexiest look on his face while he was biting his lip and looking down at me. He started pumping harder and harder. I knew he was about to cum, so I tried to back off, but he pushed his dick deeper down my throat. I felt the warm fluid hit my tongue and fall down my throat.

"Go get me a towel out the closet," he barked. "Damn, you got spit all over my fucking pants."

I ran over to the first door, and when I opened it, I saw a few folded towels on one of the shelves. I walked back over and he stood there waiting for me to clean him off. I got down and started wiping his pants.

"Good girl." He pulled his pants up and went to take a seat.

"Start tomorrow," he said, fixing his tie.

I started to walk out when he called out to me.

"Oh, and whatever reason you didn't want me to check you out, don't let it come up. Oh, and take this." He pulled a box out of the drawer and threw it to me. The only two words that jumped out was clit shocker. "You're required to wear that to all meetings."

I shook my head and started to regret what I had done. "I can't do that." I laughed nervously.

"You can, and I think you're gonna love it too. Take it and put it in your office drawer. If you want to stick around until I go to lunch, we can continue what we started." He smiled, and all my doubts went out the window. He was so sexy, but I could see he wasn't the type of man I would go for emotionally.

"Well, see you later?" I asked.

"You sure will."

He turned to his computer and started hitting keys. I left, feeling cheap, but fuck it. If that bitch, Tori, could fuck to get what she wanted, then so could I. I had just landed a job with a top entertainment law firm, and I was on my way up.

I was going to be as successful and put together as Donathon remembered when he fell in love with me as Rita. Now I needed to make him fall for Ellie.

"So, when is she supposed to be leaving?" Monica asked me for the third time this week.

She was pissing me off because she wasn't even my girl. She was just like most of the bitches I had been running into, trying to get a quick come up. I didn't let her know that I'm hip to her shit, but if she didn't shut the fuck up, she would know soon.

"When I'm ready for her to, that's when." I grabbed my new yellow and black foams and sat on the bed to put them on.

"So, you just move some bitch in, and it's whatever, huh? That's fine. Watch me," she said, doing her theatrics, grabbing her purse and shit.

She stopped and started clapping her ass for some reason, and looking at me as if I would miss it. I shook my head and continued to ignore her ass, then got up and went to the dresser to put on some Armani cologne. I was just coming back from Florida after going to a few conferences and shit. I was leaving again soon. I missed Tori, so this was why I was trying to hang with her today.

"So, you're just gonna let me leave?" she whined.

I inhaled deeply and turned around.

"Look, I don't wanna hurt your feelings, but baby, you ain't my girl. I ain't got one, and I can have who the fuck I want in my house. Matter of fact, fuck your pussy. Now you can leave." I grabbed her jacket and tossed it to her, then made a scooting motion with my hand.

"Knock on Tori's door to make sure she's up for me," I said as I brushed my fade down and checked myself out in the mirror.

"Fuck you too, K.C.," she said as she left out.

I could tell I hurt her feelings, so I jogged to the door and called her back.

"What?" she said with this cute little defeated look on her face.

"Stop acting simple, man. I'ma call you, aight?" I smirked and kissed her on the cheek.

She started smiling, and I knew I had reeled her back in.

When I closed the door, I rolled my eyes and finished getting ready. I knew Tori wasn't asleep because I was about to take her to breakfast and to the mall. I had promised her she wouldn't spend all day in the house because I wouldn't let her. My staff had told me she had been in the house all day since I'd been gone. I hated how she felt about herself, and I was doing everything I could to make her feel special. See, her fucking for money wasn't surprising to me because of who my parents were.

My father used to pimp, and my mother was one of his hoes. They never hid that fact from me, my brother, Anderson, and our sister, Lexi. My mother wasn't like the other bitches though, she was smart, and she was only doing the shit to take care of Anderson. He was her first born, and the nigga she had him by was married and didn't want shit to do with her or Anderson. She started stripping first, then she slowly turned to tricking and shit.

She met my father, and he peeped that she wasn't like most bitches, fucking to get high and shit. So, he sent her to school and shit. She graduated and he wifed her ass. He wasn't even sending her out anyway because in my mind, he already knew he wanted her from jump street. That's how I feel about Tori. She's too good to be out here doing this dumb shit, that's why I didn't judge her. Sometimes you got to do what you got to do.

I knew she wasn't no hoe, and I knew that she was loyal as fuck to a nigga she called hers. I felt bad for her when that nigga stepped off on her and shit. What kind of bitch ass nigga would leave his girl in a hospital all fucked up? That's all good, though. If he didn't want shawty, I would damn sure sit her up on a pedestal.

I grabbed my phone and headed down to her room to see if she was ready. I already knew she wasn't asleep when I said that shit to Monica because I was texting her while I was in the shower. When I got closer, I could hear arguing, and I wanted to fuck Monica up. When I walked in, she was all in Tori's face talking shit.

"Bitch, you think you're real fuckin' smart, huh? That nigga is mine, so take your crippled ass the fuck on," she said, poking Tori in the head.

Tori put on a fucked-up smile, and the shit looked downright scary. Monica tried to back up, but it was too late. Tori smacked her right across the face with the cane.

"You bitch!" Monica got up and tried to attack her, but I pushed her out the way.

"Tell her to leave now, K.C.," Monica yelled at me.

I picked up my phone while looking at Tori.

"Come up to the second room on the left," I told security.

"Good, now pack your lil shit up, bitch," Monica said, still adding fuel to the fire.

"Sir?" my lead security, Broc said as he walked in.

"Yeah, get this bitch out my house." I pointed at Monica.

Her mouth hung open, and she started swinging at Broc.

"I told your dumb ass to stop tripping, man. Don't make me turn up on yo ass either. Come on, boo, you ready?" I asked Tori with my hand out.

I could hear Monica cursing and threatening me and shit. Simple bitch.

"So, we just gon act like that bitch ain't stupid?" Tori asked, getting up.

"No, I know the bitch dumb, but I ain't 'bout ta let her fuck up your day."

Tori no longer wanted to use her cane since she was walking a lot better. She kept it next to the bed in case it was some middle of the night shit and she wasn't feeling strong.

"Well, if I'm causing personal problems—"

"Shut that shit up, man. I'm hungry as hell and ready to go."

She smiled, and I couldn't help but kiss her on the lips. I caught her off guard. I could tell by how she touched her lips when I pulled back.

"K.C.," she whispered.

"Yeah, I know," I said and walked away.

"What is it you know? I'm recovering. I don't want you to be a rebound where I only love you out of convenience. Don't you want me to love you because I really love you, not because you saved me?"

She made sense, but I had been patient, and I guess it's just not there.

"You right bae, damn. You ready?" I asked again.

"I am." She grabbed her purse and I set it back down.

"You won't need it."

I smiled and we walked out the room. I couldn't lie and say I wasn't crushed that I would probably never get to make her happy the way I want because she was loving another nigga. Didn't mean I couldn't still treat her the way I think she should be treated.

I couldn't wait to eat, and I wanted to surprise her with something I didn't let her know about yet. We pulled into a diner with large blue letters that read. *Bonnie's Place.*

"I hope they got blueberry pancakes," Tori said, walking around the car with me.

"I'm think they do. And some strawberry shit too, I liked those." I opened the door for her and she walked in and smiled.

"I love this, how come I've never seen this place?" she said, looking around at the 60s-retro styled setup.

"Two, please," I told the hostess.

She looked confused, but seated us anyway.

"Your waiter will be with you." The older woman smiled and walked away.

"Oh look!" Tori said, picking up the menu and showing me the stack of fruit pancake choices.

"I'm def about to go in, shawty."

My cousin Charmaine walked up with a stupid smile on her face.

"You funny as fuck, boy," Charmaine said, coming in and hugging me.

"Hi," she said, looking at Tori.

"Hello." Tori smiled.

"So, you not going to introduce me to your woman, boy?" Charmaine put her hands on her hips.

"She not my girl, that's why. This is my friend, Tori." I motioned toward Tori. "Tori, this is my cousin, Charmaine."

They shook hands.

"So, you know I could have just whipped y'all up something real fast, and since you own the place, why you acting like a regular person?" She laughed and shook her head.

"Damn, what else did I miss?" Tori said.

"Oh, chile, come on, let me tell you about him." She grabbed Tori's hand and walked her to the back.

I couldn't imagine what she was telling her, but I could hear them cackling all the way up front.

"So, that's her, huh?" I heard my mother say.

I looked up and smiled because after she sat us down, she nodded in approval.

"Yup, gorgeous, ain't she?" I smiled.

"She definitely is. So, is she doing okay?" she asked. I had told my mother all about Tori, even the fact she used to get with Anderson while she was working.

"She okay, I just know I got to let her go. She don't want me, Ma. She wants that bitch nigga who left her on stupid," I said, shaking my head.

"You got to give her a chance to heal, baby boy. You can't just expect her to get over this type of devastation and just be happy. I bet if you fall back, she will see you, I promise." She smiled.

"I guess. I wanna know why you here though, now that I think about it. I told you this was for you, that don't mean you got to be hosting and stuff." I had hired her enough staff that she wouldn't need to come and do shit like that.

"I want to. I ain't got nothing to do in that big ass house with your father snoring in my damn face all day. I wanna be here." She grabbed my hand.

"Oh, my God, I'm clowning you for days." Tori came out smiling with a plate in her hand.

"Charmaine, you irritating. I swear," I shot at her.

"Tori, nice to finally meet you," my mother said, breaking up the conversation.

"Nice to meet you too," Tori said, unsure of who it was nice to meet.

"I'm his mother." Ma laughed.

"Oh okay, I knew something was up when we came in. How you looked at him let me know." Tori hugged her.

"Now it's my turn." She pulled Tori to the side, and just like before, I sat at the table and waited to be embarrassed.

"I like her, cuzo," Charmaine said, looking over at Tori and my mother.

"I do too, I wish she felt like that," I said as I looked over at the two of them myself.

"She does, she told me how y'all met in class and how she only thought you was being nice to her to get her answers." She giggled.

Tori looked over at me and smiled. That nigga didn't deserve her, I did.

Four months had passed since I moved into K.C.'s house, and his therapy team had done wonders. I was lonely as hell, but besides that, I was okay. Honestly, my heartbreak wasn't completely gone, but I knew it wasn't shit I could do about my past' I damn sure was fixing my future, though. I had my degree, despite how graduation had gone. I had money, and plenty of it. Now it was time to figure out what I was gonna do with myself. I was walking fine now, but I still had that stiffness in my arm. I had to have my hair cut down because I slid and my head dragged, but I was looking like me again.

I knew it would be time for me to leave soon, so I called the utility companies and told them I needed my services back on. I couldn't say I wouldn't miss spending every day with K.C., but I knew I had to move out so he could continue his life.

Today was the perfect day to do it because he was at his training camp. I was, of course, gonna tell him I was leaving, but I knew that if I did before I left, he would try to get me to stay. He deserved to live free and not worry about me, so I was removing myself.

"You know he is gonna come looking, right?" my mother said while carrying my bags down the stairs.

"He won't have to look, I'm gonna tell him I'm gone. He's not my man, Ma," I said as I threw my duffle in the trunk. I only called her because, of course, I haven't driven my own car since before the graduation.

"I'm just saying, sweetheart, look around you. This man is what you need, not some piece of shit who left you to die in a hospital," she screamed.

"And you're just so fucking helpful bringing that shit up. I know white women like you prey on rich black men, just like how you did my father, but please don't try to make me into you," I said and rolled my eyes.

"Listen to me, you little bitch. You don't know shit about what the fuck I had to do to stay married to that son of bitch Marcus. He was a low down cheating dog, and I stayed for you! So you could have a family, then he leaves after sucking my soul dry, and now here you are trying to judge me? Fuck you too, Tori." She pulled my bags out her car and threw them on the ground.

"I just want you to be happy, I want you to have what I didn't. A man who loves you. That boy loves you, Tori. Your head is so shoved up your ass, you can't see shit but Donathon."

She got in her car and drove off on my ass. That was the first time I felt like I was wrong in a long time. Look how she treated me, though. What the fuck? She never even said sorry for her racist ass boyfriend who dumped her ass for some hood rat. The nerve. I called her and she surprisingly picked up.

"What!" she yelled into the phone.

"I'm sorry, Mom. Can you come back?" I cried into the phone.

"Why should I, Tori? You want me out of your life so bad, you got it."

She hung up, and I threw my phone on the ground. I needed to get my life because I was fucking up and pushing everybody away because of how I felt. My phone rang and I just knew it was her calling back, so I went and picked my phone up. It was K.C.

"Hey," I answered like nothing was wrong.

"Damn shawty, you was trying to leave without saying nothing, huh?" He laughed into the phone.

"What?" I asked, wondering how he knew.

"Stop playing. Mario gonna drive you, okay?" he said.

"Thank you, K.C.," I said, feeling once again like a burden.

"No problem. Hit me when you get in, aight, so I can know you good."

"I will. So, how's training."

"K.C! Hurry up, baby." I heard a female voice through the phone.

"I got to go, ma. Hit me, aight?" He hung up and I saw a black Expedition pull up into the driveway, so I moved out the way.

I wondered who the girl was on the phone rushing him off with me. Not my business, I guess. I waited for Mario to get his ass out the car and help me, but it wasn't him who stepped out. It was two official looking people, and it scared the shit out of me. One was tall, and he looked like Damon Wayons, and the other was short and he looked like Tattoo from *Fantasy Island*.

"Hi, we're looking for a Miss Tori Minors," Damon Wayon's twin stated.

They both pulled out their badges, and I started to get sick.

"What's wrong?" I asked, now needing to know why they were here.

"I'm Detective Samson, and this is my partner, Detective Gunther. Hope you don't mind, but we got your forwarded address from the post office."

I was getting impatient.

"Okay, and? What is it?" I asked.

"Do you know a Donathon Gray?" Tattoo asked.

"Yes, he's my ex-boyfriend," I said, getting worried that something had happened to him. I was so stupid. Worried of a nigga who left me stupid.

"Well, we saw you two had a history, and you even got locked up together when you were teens."

"Okay, so what the hell do you want?" I leaned to the side and tapped my foot, letting them know their time was close.

"We found a vehicle that was used in a robbery homicide, and we have Mr. Gray's fingerprints, and a video of him getting out of the car. We also have this," he said and pulled out a tablet to show me a car pulling up, and me standing at my car.

"Hold up, I know the fuck y'all not trying to say me or him had shit to do with a bank robbery. How the hell do you know that's even him in the car? You know what, bye. Lock me up or leave me the fuck alone," I said, feeling unsettled.

I remember that day. I was about to go to the bank when some car pulled up and this masked man stared me down. No way that could have been him, he wouldn't have kept that from me. Especially not how he went off about me keeping my secret. That motherfucker! I was furious with him, and myself as well. I never asked how he had so much money, and I'd never seen him go to work or even say shit about work. I should have known.

"Well, play tough if you want, but standing by your man won't work this time."

They turned around and went back to the car. I couldn't believe him, now who had the secrets?

Mario finally showed up and drove me to my house. When I got inside, it was so empty, I wanted to cry. I was alone again, by choice, I guess. The walk to my bedroom brought back memories of when I first brought it. Donathon helped me choose my wall paints and everything. He was all over this house. I actually thought about calling him, but decided against it. What would that do? I lay back on my bed and just thought about everything that happened. Where the hell did I go wrong?

My phone rang, and I saw a number that surely had to call me by mistake. I wasn't sure if I should answer it or not, but my curiosity got the better of me.

"Why are you calling me?" I yelled at Jackson.

"I just wanted you to know you were right to do what you did. My wife divorced me, and it made me realize I couldn't be mad at anybody but myself. I'm sorry for hurting you, Tori. I'm not trying to get back with you or nothing like that, but I just wanted you to know how truly sorry I was."

This had to be a joke. I hung up and threw my phone on the charger. I giggled and went downstairs to grab a menu to order me something to eat and made a mental to make sure I hit the grocery store tonight. I wanted to wake up to some damn breakfast like at K.C.'s house. He had the cooks make me whatever I wanted every single morning. Damn, I was stupid, now that I think about it. That man treated me like a queen, even when I didn't deserve it.

I had liked K.C at one point, and of course, the only reason the crush died was because I was with Don. I was surprised to get a text soon after from K.C. I figured he would be busy with whoever the bitch was who called out to him. We texted the whole night, and at 2:00 in the morning, his ass video called me to make sure I didn't have no nigga in the bed with me. I couldn't help but laugh at his simple ass. He asked me on a date, but he wouldn't set one. He said it's a surprise.

I wasn't going to rush into anything serious right now, but shit a date or two to be a distraction wouldn't hurt.

****

"You look nice today," the trainer at the sports medicine center told me while I did leg stretches.

K.C. had set it up for me to get seen here. I had seen so many celebrity players that I wasn't star struck anymore.

"Thank you," I said as I pushed my leg back as far as it could go.

"So, you got a man?" he asked.

"No," I said flatly.

"Damn, what stupid nigga fucked up?"

"Look, I think its unprofessional for you to be hitting on me while I'm trying to get better."

"Yeah, it really is," I heard K.C chime in.

"I was ju—"

"Yeah, I know what you were just doing." K.C. came up and hugged me.

"I'm sorry. Please don't tell my boss. My baby mother trippin' and shit, and I can't lose this job." The therapist was pleading.

"Yeah, whatever." K.C turned to flash that magazine ready smile.

"Why are you here?" He didn't tell me he was coming into town.

"Damn, you want me to stay gone?" he said, holding his hands up as to say 'whats up?'

"I just didn't know you were heading back. A few days ago, you were partying and shit," I said with a smirk.

"Look at you clocking me and shit." He smiled.

"Ain't nobody clockin' you, boy."

I saw a few of the patients stopping to look at the TV, so I walked closer to see what all the fuss was about. I almost threw up when I saw Donathon's picture flash across the screen as wanted for questioning in a murder and bank robbery. *Oh my God.*

One Month Later

It was time for me to get my hair done because K.C. and I were going on a date tonight, and I wanted to look my best. I was going to the Dominicans to get my shit laid. I pulled to the end of the block and got out, grabbing my oversized bag with me. I didn't really like this part of town, but it was where you could get your hair laid, nails slayed, and lashes pumped.

I walked past all the girls who I was sure were working, and thought about myself. *At least I wasn't out here like this.* I thought.

"Tori," a weak voice called out to me.

I looked to my left, and I couldn't control the tears of pity that fell from my eyes.

"Larrise. What happened to you?" I asked.

She looked so bad, the only way I could tell it was her was her eyes.

"I'm still having a little trouble," she said.

"I thought you went back home?" I asked as I looked at her.

She had on a pair of dirty shorts, a bra, and a pair of old tennis shoes.

"I did, but I love me some Houston," she said, shaking her ass. "You got any money?" she asked, coming toward me.

This time, I was ready for her ass.

"No, you need to get some fucking help, Larrise. You look like shit," I said and walked off.

"You was fucking for money too, bitch, so don't sit here all high and mighty. That's why your ass got what you got at graduation." She laughed.

I started laughing too. "Chile, please, I don't even think about that. See, look at me and look at you. You're out here fucking any Tom, Dick and Harry for ten bucks, when I was making top dollar for a taste of this pussy. I got a NBA star on my line. Yeah, you remember K.C., right? I'm sure you do, so that little stunt didn't stop shit. I'm still better than you, Larrise."

I rolled my eyes and she grabbed my arm. I took my mace out and sprayed her right in the eyes.

"I can't see," she screamed and rolled on the dirty ground.

"And as for graduation and that shit at my apartment..." I kicked her in the face two times. "Fuck, you bitch!"

I spit on her and walked down to the salon and preceded to get my hair done. Stupid bitch.

*****

"Damn, I know I said look your best, but shit, shawty." K.C. whirled me around.

I had on my new jumper dress with a brand-new pair of high top Jordans. My hair was beautifully blown out, and I wore a small pair of butterfly earrings

"Thank you." I smiled, trying to cheer up.

That news report had fucked me up emotionally, and K.C was being a sweetheart and taking me out on a surprise date. He had spent the last month with me, and he was giving me those love butterflies. It was undeniable. I felt like I should be worried about Don, but he wasn't worried about my ass when I needed him, so fuck it. I just needed to lift my spirits, and K.C. was giving me life. I couldn't wait to see where we would end up.

"You got anything you always wanted to do?" he asked, grabbing my purse for me.

"I don't know, you can start by taking me to eat."

"I can do that and more."

He put his hand on the small of my back and walked me outside. My ass was stuck when I saw a pink closed carriage attached to two beautiful white horses sitting in my driveway.

"Boy." I jumped into his arms.

"Yeah, now you all on a nigga." He laughed.

"Come on." I ran down to where the footman held the door open.

When I got inside, I screamed. It was lit up with a blue light that shadowed the entire carriage, and there was a TV facing the soft, plush seats.

"Pour up, ma." K.C. hit a button and the lower wall dropped, revealing a mini bar behind it. He poured us two glasses of champagne and handed me one.

"To me putting a smile on your face." We clanked glasses and I sipped it.

"This is amazing." I was still taken aback.

"Go!" K.C Yelled to the men guiding us.

They pulled off, and I watched the ground move. This was so dope.

"So, where are we going?" I inquired while sipping from my glass.

"Somewhere that you can't run from." He smiled and grabbed my thigh.

I tightened my legs because he made my pussy tingle when he touched my skin.

"I'm not running from you." I rolled my eyes.

"Well, let me make you feel good, ma." He closed the visors on both sides of the carriage.

"What?" I asked, wondering why we needed to be closed in.

"Let me just taste it." He licked his lips and stared down at my pelvic area.

I started to blush and shook my head. "You not gonna stop there, so no." I looked at the TV, watching the BET commercial about the upcoming awards.

"You ain't watching that shit." He picked up the remote and turned the channel to a music station.

I got your legs spread all over the bed, hands gripping the sheets, hair wild as hell I know, the only thing on your mind is sexing me.

My heart was pounding so fast because I wasn't ready for sex with him. I didn't want to keep giving my body to get broken in return.

"I think we should just stop," I said as he kissed my chest. At the same time, he was tracing his hand up my jumper. I gasped when I felt his fingers circling my clit.

"You want me to lick it? Say yes."

He was sucking on my ear lobe and using his free hand to play with my nipples. I could feel the buggy stop, and thought I was saved from giving up the pussy, but I guess it was just a red light.

I had to admit the sounds of the car engines, radios, and people talking turned me on. They had no idea what we were doing back here.

"I got to eat it." He got down, and I felt a rough tug as he ripped my underwear off.

"Oh my God!" I was feeling him and he was only licking the inside of my thighs.

My toes curled when he kissed me on the back of my knees and licked all the way to the meeting of my thighs.

"I knew you would smell like this, boo."

I could feel my lips part and his warm thick tongue licked my clit. He threw my legs over his shoulders and ate my pussy like I never felt. He was probing in and out of my opening, and the fact that he was moaning like he was enjoying it more than I was.

"Kadeem! Oh God!" I called that nigga by his government, he was killing the pussy with his tongue alone.

"Cum in my mouth, boo," he said before pulling my clit into his mouth.

"I'm not ready." I cried, literally. I was in tears from his head game.

"Yes, you are."

He stuck two fingers inside me and continued to lap my pussy up. I felt my nut building, and he must have sensed it because he flipped me over and spread my ass cheeks. He didn't waste any time eating the groceries. He bounced his tongue in and out my ass hole as he pushed his face into my ass and jiggled my ass cheeks on his face. He was licking me from pussy to ass, and I gripped the back of the seat and faced the back window that didn't have a visor.

There was a woman in the car behind us, and she must have

caught on to what was going on. My faces were probably a dead giveaway. I thought she was about to pull away. but she licked her finger and slid it down. I couldn't even react to her because K.C. had my clit in his mouth again, and this time, I was about to blow.

"I'm about to cum, baaaabbbyyyy."

"Cum then." He stuck a finger in and I shot nut all down his hands and in his face, I'm sure.

"Shit, girl."

K.C. got up and went to the mini bar, then pulled a towel from a small opening and cleaned himself up. He grabbed me one and started to clean me off. He even grabbed a bottle of water, saturated the towel, and wiped me down.

"That was unexpected." I turned in the seat and fixed my clothes.

"I expected it. I been planning it since I met you," he said as he cleaned his face with a wipe.

"You so nasty." I covered my face.

"Wait 'til you ready for the dick, ma. I get real nasty." He licked out his tongue and waved it.

"Ugh." I laughed and pushed him.

He opened the side windows back and pointed. "Look at that."

I looked out and saw a huge air balloon sitting in a field.

"That's for us?" I smiled.

"Damn right."

The grass had lights streaming a makeshift walk way to the air balloon. When I got on, it was way bigger than I imagined. There was a table for two set up, and two trays with metal covering. In the corner stood a white girl dressed in a female tuxedo, and she was holding a bottle of Pierre noir.

K.C. pulled my chair out, and we both sat down while we lifted off. I was kinda scared, thinking that whatever was holding this thing from floating off was gonna let go. The girl poured us two glasses and she pulled the covers off the food.

"What the hell?" It was only a cup of chocolate syrup in mine, and a bowl of whip cream in his.

"I wasn't done." He got down and pulled my shoe off.

"Stop, you don't see her right there?" I pointed.

"Turn the fuck around," he barked at her.

She did what he said and looked off into the sky.

"Are you fuc—"

I was cut off by him sucking whipped cream off my toes. I tried not to make a noise, but he was determined to make me scream. After a few minutes, my legs were up, and he was pouring chocolate down my pussy and eating me for dessert just like he said.

When he came up, he had chocolate all over his face. He kissed me, and I could taste myself on his tongue. The rest of the night, he took me to different places and ate my pussy wherever we went. At the restaurant in the manager's office, then we went to a play just so he could drag me into the back and lock us in a changing room. Those people banged on the door until we came out. We laughed all the way out the building.

"You're fucking crazy, you know that?"

"Crazy about your ass," he said in a serious tone.

"I'm starting to feel the same way," I said honestly.

"So, you saying you ready for us?" he asked.

"I will be soon, I just need more time. We can date, can't we?"

I didn't wanna jump straight into another relationship, and to be honest, I felt that he was the one who wasn't as ready as we should be.

"Yeah, I don't mind taking your light ass out."

He swooped me up and started running. I screamed with excitement as we made it to a small ice cream shop. He had a smirk on his face.

"No, no, I can't take no more."

I went in kicking and screaming, but it didn't do shit. He was hungry.

Donathon

I was staying in a hotel right outside of North Carolina, and I was dog tired from driving the last five hours straight. This was the third place I had stopped in the last month. I warmed up my burger from McDonalds and lay back on the bed. I never got back up because when my head hit the bed, I was gone.

It was morning when I opened my eyes, and I was still fully dressed down to my shoes. The sun was beaming right in my face, and I got up and kicked my shoes off. I had bought a burner cell to call my family in DC. I'd heard the radio saying I was wanted for questioning, and it made me sick as fuck. They had to have something to want me to come in and talk. I didn't want to be on the run, so I figured I would get a lawyer to find out what they were talking about before I took my ass in there.

I took out my phone to call my cousin Drama, he was supposed to meet me here since he lived about ten minutes from where I was. I knew he would come quickly.

"Cuzzo," I said after he answered.

"Wassup, bruh. You here?" he asked.

"Yeah. 105. Bring me something good, man. You know I need it," I said and hung up.

I needed to smoke. I didn't even smoke like that, but I knew that shit would give me a 'fuck it' attitude and ease my mind a little bit. There was a shitty gas station in the parking lot of the motel, so I went to grab some Backwoods and some candy. I was hungry as fuck, so as soon as I smoked, I was gonna grab some food from the Waffle House I passed around the corner. I started walking back to my room when I saw some chocolate thick joint walking into the ice and vending machine area.

Some pussy didn't sound like a bad idea right now. I wished I could stop thinking about Tori for a minute to actually go through with fucking somebody else. I know I told her we couldn't be together right now, and I meant the shit. I still loved that girl like my last breath, but I needed to think. On some real shit, though, I wish I could dig that motherfucker Jaden up. I ain't Ray Charles, that nigga raped her, and I couldn't blame her for that. I would never want to.

I went and pissed on that nigga's grave a few days after the shit at the graduation. I just didn't understand why she ain't tell me. Who's to say how I would have reacted, but I know it would have been a lot different than what happened. I woulda whooped Jaden's ass for her. I would have killed him myself if I knew he had been doing that shit to her. It's pissing me off to even think about it.

"You need help?" the girl said.

I didn't realize I had been standing there for a while, just thinking.

"Oh, yeah. I was just waiting for somebody," I lied and started walking toward my room.

"Too bad, I saw when you checked in. My mother owns this shit hole, so I see everybody who comes in and out."

She was cute as hell too, a gap between her front two teeth, but she was nice with it.

"Cuzzo!" Drama yelled out the window of his old ass 1993

Buick.

This nigga had duct tape holding the trunk closed from what I can see. I couldn't believe this nigga had what looked like 22s on this raggedy motherfucker. It barely had paint. When I walked around to the passenger side, he had a rope hanging out the door. I was embarrassed for him.

"Wassup, fool." I shook my head and walked over to him.

"Nothin', nigga. Pull the rope to open the door," he yelled.

"Nigga just park and meet me at the room."

The girl had walked off by now, so I went to the room and waited for this fool.

There was a knock on the door, and I told Drama to come in. The door opened, and when I looked up, it wasn't Drama. It was her.

"Your cousin said he had to run, and he asked me if I could give you this," she said, walking up and handing me a nice ass zip.

"Thanks," I said as I grabbed it from her. "You smoke?"

"Yeah, sometimes." She came and sat down next to me. "So, what you doing alone in a hotel room? You must be stopping through?"

"What your name?" I asked, completely ignoring her question.

"Rain." She slipped her braid back.

I closed the Backwood and lit it up.

"You know these are non-smoking rooms," Rain said.

"So."

I passed it to her and she pulled deep. As soon as she started choking violently, I knew she didn't smoke that much.

"What's your name?" she asked as she laid back and got comfortable.

"D."

"Well, it's not a lot of nice looking men who come through here."

She placed her leg behind my back, which gave me a nice view of between her legs. Her skirt was up to her thighs. Shawty was bold as shit. She started rubbing her pussy over top of her pink underwear.

"You don't even know me," I said, pulling on the tree, and pretending to be unfazed by her little show.

My dick was ready to bust through my jeans. Her chocolate ass thighs alone had me ready to push into that pussy.

"So? There's condoms. Don't tell me you scared of pussy, D."

She continued to play with herself until she stopped to lift her legs and pull her underwear off. Damn. Fuck it. I put the weed down and got right between her legs. I basically ripped her shirt off, and when her titties fell out, I immediately jumped on her Hershey's Kiss nipples.

"Oh God, that feels so good." She moaned while wrapping her legs around me.

"I don't have no condoms. I got to run to the gas station again." I tried to get up, but she pulled me back down.

"I got you." I heard paper rattling as she pulled a Magnum out her bra.

She must do this shit a lot.

I got up and got undressed before rolling the condom down on my dick. She had her legs open and ready when I came down and worked my way into her pussy. She was nice and tight, too.

"I knew you had a big dick," she screamed.

I was entranced because she felt so good, a nigga was feeling weak as shit. I had to get my mind off how good this pussy was before I fucked up and nut quick.

"Come here."

I pulled her up and pulled the chair from under the table. I had to hurry up and switch positions so I could reset. I set her on her knees facing the back of the chair. Her ass wasn't huge, but it was nice. I was loving how my dicked looked going in and out of her.

"Yeeees, D."

She threw her head back and started to throw it back, but I could tell she couldn't take the dick like she was pretending to. Every time I went deep, her back came up, and she tried to pull away. Tori used to do that too. *Fuck!* I thought. Why the fuck did I have to think of her? My dick started to get soft after guilt kicked in.

"What wrong?" Rain turned around to ask.

"Nothing. I forgot I have to do some shit real quick." I turned around and pulled the condom off.

"So, it wasn't good or something? You kinda hurting my feelings," she said with her voice cracking.

"It's not that. I got a lot of shit going on, and I can't focus. It was good as fuck, ma. My dick was hard when I saw you. It's not you, I promise." I looked at her, hoping to make her feel better, but I could tell that I hadn't.

"That's fine." As she snatched her shoes up, she looked so embarrassed.

She stormed out the room before I could say anything else to her. Another broad that hates a nigga. I picked up my weed and kept smoking. I could still smell her perfume and pussy on me. I wish I could have at least bust a nut. I ran to the Waffle House and grabbed my food to go.

When I got back, I ate while watching one of the six channels they had on the TV. I lucked up, and *Life* came on. This was some chill shit to look at. I thought maybe I should go find Rain and try to pick up where we left off, but I ended up going my ass to bed early as fuck any way.

Before I could even open my eyes fully, the door flew off the hinges and a team of mufuckas with the word U.S Marshal across their vests were over me with guns.

"Get down!" They pulled me out of bed and cuffed me.

How the fuck would they know I was here?

When they were walking me out the door, I got my answer when I saw Rain crying to one of the niggas.

"Yes, I saw the news yesterday and I went to his room to confront him about being wanted. He tried to beat me up to keep me quiet," she told him.

"Bitch, you came to fuck, and your pussy was so whack my dick went soft," I screamed over my shoulder while they dragged me away.

That stupid hoe, fuck it.

****

The ride back to Texas was some bullshit. I started to piss on the floor because these bitch ass niggas refused to stop. I'm sure that shit had to be against the law. When they took me into the courthouse, people where holding their noses because of the strong piss smell I carried when I passed them.

"What the fuck, man?" a white bald head officer said when I

was sat down.

"Motherfucka pissed in the back to teach us a lesson," one of my transporters said.

"Mr. Gray, I've been looking for you," some fat nigga walked up and said. "Detective Gunther," he introduced himself with his hand extended.

I had cuffs on, so I laughed at how stupid the nigga was being right now. He walked me to a room, and I sat in the chair. He uncuffed one hand and sat across from me.

"What the fuck y'all want?" I already knew why I was there, but it wouldn't help to pretend to be clueless.

"We got you, cut the shit. Your lil friend didn't do good covering you guys' tracks. We got phone records, prints, videos. You're done, and you get to eat the shit alone."

He tapped his hand on the table.

"Lawyer," I said, then leaned back in my chair.

"You can—"

"LAWYER!" I yelled, cutting him off.

"Another nigga in prison," he said before getting up and leaving.

A few minutes later, the door opened and a cute Spanish joint walked in and set her briefcase down.

"I'm your lawyer. You didn't tell them anything, did you?" she asked.

"No, I didn't tell them shit. Who hired you? I didn't," I told her.

"Well, let's just say you got friends, okay? News of your arrest didn't sit well, so here I am."

What friends was this bitch talking about?

"Let me say they cannot hold you. They lied about all the evidence being clear. They are waiting for a few other things that can nail you to the wall."

"Okay, so when can I leave?" I asked.

"I'm working on it now," she said.

She stopped and looked at me strangely.

"You good?" I snapped.

"Yeah, I'm fine. I will be back in about an hour." She walked out and I picked up the card she left on the desk.

Ellie Santia, I said in my head. I didn't give a fuck who her sexy ass was, as long as she got me out of there.

K.C.

I was home for a while since the season was about to start up. I was nervous as fuck for my first professional game too. Of course, I knew I had skills, but the fact that it was millions of people watching me had me sick. I knew as long Tori was there, I would be okay though, I just needed to ask her. Now some might say I seemed press for her, but I swear she so fucking attractive in every sense of the word. She was never pressed to be on my dick lie most bitches were, and I fucked with that shit hard as fuck.

I'd liked her since the day I met her. That shy shit made my dick hard, and every time I talked to her and she did that nervous laugh, she stole a nigga's heart. I've been thinking about when I ate the pussy all night. I could do that shit every day if she would let me. I wanted to hit her spot in the worst way, but by the look on her face I could tell she wasn't ready for all of that. I always kept my control whenever I was close to her, but I was itching for her.

We'd been doing that white people dating shit. Like I told her, I didn't mind, but I wanted more. I wanted to cuff her ass. My dick started to get hard thinking about her, and I started rubbing it. I decided to nudge Ciara, she was one of my regular joints. I liked her more than any broad I ever called myself talking to besides Tori. She wasn't gold digging either because she had her own money.

"What, K.C.?" she said, stirring around.

"Gimme some pussy, girl. Open them legs." I got up and started pulling her legs apart." She kept them locked, but I got them open.

"Dammit, you and your nasty dreams. Keep waking up horny and shit."

I ignored her while I ran a condom down my dick and pushed in. She was screaming after only three strokes.

"Damn, boy." She moaned.

I wanted her to turn away for real because she had just woken up, and her breath was smelling like hot shit. I was imagining myself fucking Tori, which made me beat her pussy up. I pulled one of her legs up and held on to the top of the bed, and dug into that pussy like a crazy nigga. Ciara was screaming bloody murder, but I kept digging that shit out. I felt my nut building up after ten minutes of crushing her pussy. I came hard as fuck, then pulled the condom off and went to the bathroom to flush it.

"Good morning to you too." Ciara laughed.

"I got to hop in the shower real fast, grab me something to wear." I told her as I turned the lever for the hot water.

"Bossy ass."

She got up and went to do what I told her. I hit the built in mp3 on the wall and played some Kevin Gates.

"Baby," Ciara called out.

"Yeah?" I said, washing my dick off.

"Who is Tori?"

"Why?" I asked, pulling the glass door back.

"Because she called you, then sent you a text about meeting up today." She was leaned to the side, holding my phone like she caught me.

"First of all, put my phone down before I fuck you up, and second, none of your damn business."

I closed the door and finished my shower. That was some shit I didn't play. I didn't go through her shit, and since she wasn't my girl, I wouldn't have a reason to. When you give some of these females dick, they think you go together, even though you tell them you ain't going that way. I shook my head and got out the shower and dried off. When I walked out, she was getting dressed. I could tell she was crying, so I went up and tried to hug her, but she pushed me off.

"Why can't I be enough? I got my own, I don't ask you for shit, and I treat you good, even though now I see you don't deserve it." She had tears running down her face.

"Look, man. I already told you not to put you all into me, didn't I? Now you blaming me because you hurt yourself. I like coolin' with you and everything, but you cant be like this," I said and handed her a tissue. "I ain't no ruthless motherfucker, but my word is my word. If I said you was just my lil piece, then that's what it was. I ain't gonna change my mind about the shit."

"So, this Tori girl is the one for you, huh?"

I shrugged. "She could be," I said as I put on the clothes she laid out.

"Then why you fuckin' me huh?" she started to get hype.

"Because I like pussy, shawty, duh. But look though, I got to bounce." I grabbed some socks out the drawer.

"You know what? Fine. I can get a nigga easy. Call that bitch next time you need to cum." She grabbed her shit and walked out.

"Aye," I called after her.

"What?" She walked back in.

"I'ma call you tomorrow, aight?"

I blew her a kiss and she rolled her eyes. She was gonna answer. She wasn't fooling me with all that shit she was talking. I walked out my room and heard clinking around in my kitchen. When I walked in, I shook my head at Anderson looking around in my shit like he owned it.

"Nigga, you can't knock?" I threw a table mat at the back of his head.

"Nigga, please. Don't forget who your brother is, I don't care how much money you get." He sat down and bit into the sandwich he'd just made.

"So, why do I get the pleasure of your punk ass company this morning?" I grabbed an apple out the bowl and took a bite.

"I was up the street having breakfast with a new client. I thought since your nugget head ass can't answer the phone, I would stop by. You know we got Grandma's 80th b-day in South Beach coming up, right? Pops want us there with some pretty women on our arms for the ball," he said as he wiped his hands.

"Well, you know that ain't no problem. Since you dumped your last forty bitches, who you bringing?"

"I don't know. I got this new bitch in the office, she fine as fuck, but she seems a little untrustworthy. The minute I asked about references, she dropped down to suck my dick. I knew she was hiding some shit. I'ma keep beating that pussy up until her prints come back." He laughed.

"You ain't shit, boy." I got up and dapped him up.

"Where you headed?" he asked, throwing his trash away.

"None of your business, nigga."

"I bet I know already."

"Well then don't ask." I started walking out, with him right behind me.

"Nigga, you really think you can turn a hoe—"

"Shut that shit up, nigga. I was with you when you was buying shit for the so called hoe. You see the same shit in her that I do. Cut it. Plus, I ain't gonna have to pay for it. You was business, nigga."

He was hating his ass off now.

"Fuck you too," he said as he got into his car.

I chucked him the deuce and rolled out to head to Tori.

I missed her like a motherfucker, that's why I was about to ask her to go with me to my grandmother's party right now. It would be nice to get her to the beach and shit so she could relax. Of course, I never get told no, but she was different, and I knew I just couldn't boss her around like I could do most broads. Just in case, though, I rented a house right on the beach so she could wake up to that view. I did that shit while I was driving.

She needed a break from Texas, and it ain't shit like South beach to unwind. I pulled up in front of her house and hopped out the car. I could tell she'd had gardeners there recently because it smelled like horse shit and the plants looked fresh.

As the doorbell chimed, I could hear the small footsteps approaching. The lock turned, and when Tori opened the door, my mouth dropped. She had on a robe, but it was open, and she was completely ass naked under it. She realized what I was staring at and closed it, then turned red. Her hair was dripping wet like she had just got out the pool.

"Fuck this," I said before I grabbed her by her neck and pulled her into a kiss.

I scooped her up and wrapped her legs around me.

"K.C., what are you doing."

She moaned as I grabbed her wet hair and kept kissing her. I know I had just smashed shorty, but I cleaned up and shit.

"You just got out the pool?" I pulled her robe off and started sucking her left nipple.

"We can't," she moaned, all while grabbing my head and smashing my face into her titties.

"Yes, we can. You ready for it, ma."

I picked her up and carried her out back by the pool. She had these large square pool side beds, so I laid her on one of them.

"You're gonna hurt me." She pushed me back.

"I would never hurt you." I kissed her knee and started to trail kisses up her thighs.

"You all do, you're gonna love me and leave me. Just like they all do." She pushed me off again, but this time she got up.

Tori looked scared as hell. What the fuck was up with her? We were just good all this time like we were gonna be together and shit.

"Get out, K.C.," she said and pushed me toward the side of the house.

"I never did shit to you, but here we are again. You need to get your fuckin' head checked. We was just sending kissy faces and shit, now you on this bullshit again. Fuck this shit, shawty. You ain't tryna be happy, you like being miserable as fuck, apparently. I'ma holla at you later." I shook my head and walked out the front.

"It's not that I wanna be miserable." I heard her feet stepping through the grass to catch up with me.

"Then why the fuck you can't just let me make you feel like something? I'm trying like shit, man." I leaned against the side of the house and put my head down. I ain't no weak nigga, but shawty was getting me in my feelings and shit.

"I'm sorry. I'm just scared. Your little buddy, whoever she was, sent me a picture of you in the shower after y'all fucked apparently. Is that how it's gonna be K.C.? I know we not officially together right now, but is that what I can expect? You know what? You're right. I'm not gonna be ready to trust for a while. Can I have a kiss goodbye if you're not gonna come back?" She came up, wrapped her arms around my waist, and stood on her tippy toes.

I grabbed her under the ass and pushed my tongue into her mouth. It was like I didn't hear shit she just said.

"Stop runnin'."

I turned around and pressed her against the panel. Her legs were wrapped around my waist, and I was feening to get into that pussy. I pulled my jeans down with one hand, and stroked my dick until I was all the way back hard.

"I don't have any condoms," I said, playing with her clit.

I didn't wait for an answer because I was sliding into her pussy already. Damn, I closed my eyes to enjoy the sensation that warm tightness was shooting. I knew it! I knew this pussy was amazing.

"Please don't hurt me," she cried while she came.

Damn, that was fast. Our lips touched and we breath in each other's air. The moans that she let leave her lips had me in love with this shit.

"I promise."

I covered her mouth with mine as I felt my nut building up. I planned to hit the pussy all day, so I pulled out and let it go in the grass. I could hear her breathing heavily as she leaned against me with one arm.

"My legs weak." She laughed.

"Come here."

I picked her up and we head into the house. Then, I made her scream until she fell asleep, worn the fuck out. I watched her sleep, and I don't know how many times I kissed her before I fell asleep myself.

Rita

I had no idea why I was invited on this trip with Anderson. He said he needed some work done, but I had a feeling he wanted to fuck. Now I can't complain about the dick because he is off the hood with it. But I felt like since I convinced him to let me take Donathon's case, he wants me more. I'm still very much in love with Donathon, which is why I don't want to get into anything deep, but it was hard for me to resist Anderson. He was a good distraction in the meantime.

I wasn't sure if he had a woman, but I knew a lot of the girls liked him, especially the secretaries. I put eye drops in one those bitch's drinks because she swore she was gonna have him wrapped up. I wasn't about let anybody fuck up this easy ride.

He made my work there really easy, plus I was getting good money. I hadn't really worked on a case that hard because most of them pled guilty because it was minor shit. Even though they dealt with high profile people in entertainment, they had what the employees called the scrubs department. It was for regular people who just needed a quick lawyer. I was picking up on things pretty quickly just by listening to people's conversations.

I was packing Ali's little bag so I could take him to Marline's house. She told me she would take care of him for me while I was gone next week. My bag was already packed. I had thrown a lot of sexy shit in the bag so I could blow his mind.

After I got Ali together, I went and dropped him off so I could make it in time to meet Anderson at the airport. He told me his brother and his girlfriend would be joining us. He explained that he was the brother of a NBA player; his whole family was probably successful. After kissing my little man a hundred times, I thanked Marline and got going.

When I got to the airport, I parked my car in the pay by the day and got on the shuttle. Anderson called right on time because I was getting off the shuttle.

"Hey, I'm just getting off the shuttle." I was trying to pull my suitcase down the steps, but it was stuck.

"Okay, good. It's a guy standing in front of the door next to Southwest curbside."

I walked down until I saw a small black man chilling by the door.

"Ellie?" he asked.

"Yes." He took my suitcase and I followed him.

"So, where are you?" I asked Anderson.

I looked at my phone and realized he had hung up. Rude ass. We got to TSA, and they just waved us past. That was a first. We walked down through a service door until we made it to a run way. I brushed past guys wearing jumpers and moving back and forth. There was a small airplane sitting by itself to the left. I could see Anderson through the small window, and I put a huge smile on.

They let the door down, and I climbed up the stairs and made a right to the seating. I stopped dead in my tracks when I saw that bitch Tori smiling and laughing with some guy who looked just like Anderson.

"Ellie!" Anderson called out.

"Oh, I'm sorry, hi." I shook both of their hands.

Tori was looking at me strangely, but I don't think she knew who I was.

"This is my brother Kadeem, and his girl, Tori." He motioned to them.

"Nice meeting you both." I had the fakest smile plastered on my face.

"Same."

That bitch laid back after saying that. I rolled my eyes and started talking to Anderson. He explained that we were going to his grandmother's party. I felt so honored that he would want me to meet his family. Maybe it was time for me to forget about Donathon and move on to him. He was serious about me, so maybe I should just take this new life on. Who was I kidding though? How the fuck could I pretend to be a lawyer for the rest of my life? I knew the shit wouldn't last long, but I was damn sure gonna enjoy this ride.

****

I was more than happy to get my ass of this airplane. I hated to be breathing the same air as that whore, and I was gonna make sure she suffers for life because when I got the chance, I was gonna let Kadeem know exactly who that bitch was. She thinks she can steal my husband and then go on to live well? Fuck her.

We rode to a beautiful house right in the art deco area of South Beach. I was so in love with the energy down here. I didn't bring a bathing suit, so I knew I had to go out and get me one. When we got out, I looked around at how beautiful the surroundings were. The yard was beautifully maintained, and I couldn't wait to see the inside of it.

"My brother rented one around the corner. Since you need some stuff, we all are going to the mall later once we get settled in," Anderson said, slapping my ass and walking past me to get into the house.

Ugh. I couldn't believe how small this fucking world was. Shit, this might be my chance to kill this bitch, but that might be too much right now. I would think of something. But first, let me start by figuring out how to expose this hoe.

"Listen, we're going to King of Diamonds tonight, so I want you to buy something to compete against them bitches in, aight?"

"Why am I competing? We just can't go have fun?"

"I don't remember asking you shit. I keep a bad bitch on my arm, and I don't want no bitch lookin' better than the one I have on my arm. Just do what I told you." He kissed my cheek and blasted the shower.

I could still smell his cologne even after he had been gone for a few minutes.

I pulled out a two piece black shorts romper and a pair of gold 4 inch sandal pumps. When I went to join Anderson in the shower, I heard moaning behind the door. I walked in and I saw him beating his dick in the shower to some porn on his phone. I backed out, but I had already caught his eye.

"Grab that black bag in my suitcase," he ordered.

I ran to grab what he asked and came back. He stepped out ass naked, and I felt breathless when I saw his wet, rock hard body coming toward me with a big swinging dick. He ripped my shirt off and bit into my nipple.

"Ahh," I cried out.

"You can't take it?" he looked at me as he asked with his eyes scrunched.

"Yeah, I can take it, papi."

I happily got in the shower and prepared myself for some good shit.

He grabbed my hands and quickly cuffed me to rag bar in the shower, which I didn't expect.

"What the hell is this?" I asked, feeling a little uneasy about being restrained.

He didn't answer, he just took out his next toy. It was a butt plug with some kind of remote. I watched him spit on it and come close to my ass with it. I tightened my eyes as he pushed it gently into my ass.

"This is my favorite part."

He pulled out a small wand looking object. Before I could question it, he zapped my right nipple. I jumped. Then he did the left nipple, and I screamed out because I was starting to feel the pleasure in it. I heard the switch, and the bug plug started vibrating. I was feeling sensations everywhere.

"Look how wet that pussy is, I love a freaky bitch."

He hit my clit with the wand, then tortured my body for almost thirty minutes before sliding me some dick. I was sore the whole night from what we had done. He was trying his best to enter my guts, but I was taking it like champ.

"Damn, I'ma make sure this pussy hurtin' when I'm done."

He pounded me from the back rough and savagely. That damn thing was still in my asshole and I was cumming like I never had. He finally came, and I was dead tired.

"Get up, we going shopping, remember?" Anderson pulled the cover off me.

"I wanna go to sleep now, I got some cute stuff to wear." I turned over.

"Get the fuck out the bed and get dressed now. Don't make me say the shit again," he said as he put on a pair of loafers.

"You need to watch how you talk to people," I snapped and laid back down.

I didn't hear him respond, but I felt it. The covers came off, and he was on top of me with his hand around my throat.

"I don't have tolerance for females with smart mouths, don't make me slap the shit out of you to fix that shit. Consider this a warning. I don't do well when my respect is tested."

He kissed my lips and got up. I had to make sure not to push this nigga's buttons any further. He had a short temper.

"I'm coming."

I got up and grabbed the romper I had laid out. I put on a strapless bra and zipped the front up. My titties looked like they were about to spill out. I brushed my hair over to the right side and put a pin in it. I had natural curls, so it was pretty as hell when I looked it over.

"Got damn, girl."

Anderson walked up and pushed his hand between my legs. I moaned as he massaged my clit through my shorts.

"We can pick this shit back up later." Anderson pulled away and grabbed the keys to his rental.

My phone rang while we were walking out the door. I recognize the number and got nervous.

"Hello," I anxiously answered.

"Hey, Ms. Santia, I was just checking in with you about my case," Donathon said.

"Well, I'm out of town, but I do know that trial is in about a month. I just have to grab the date. We are working really hard on your defense," I said, trying to sound professional.

"Okay cool, just let me know what's up. You know, you sound real familiar."

"I guess it's because all Spanish women sound alike." I laughed nervously.

"I guess so, talk to you later," he said and hung up.

"Who was that?" Anderson asked, opening my door for me.

"A client."

"Better be. You out here with me, and I better not hear you on the phone with another nigga, business or not."

I nodded as we drove off.

Tori

What I need from you is understanding… how can we communicate, if you don't hear what I saaaaay.

I was snapping my fingers to the beat as Xscape explained my life in that song. The bubble bath K.C had run me was taking over my senses. I couldn't believe I never pursued him. Since our first sexual encounter, he had been nothing short of amazing. We never said we were official because, of course, coming from heartache after heartache, I didn't wanna be a fool again. But he had definitely found his way into my heart.

I had my life to look forward to, and I wasn't spending any more time being sad. This trip was exactly what I needed, and I knew the fun was just starting. Last night we went out with Anderson and some awkward Hispanic girl. I noticed the way she was looking at me, and it kind of had me feeling some type of way. I didn't know what it was, but I didn't trust her. I was glad K.C. decided to drive us to the party instead of us driving with them.

"You ready, boo?" K.C came up and smiled. He was admiring my sundress as much as I was. "You look beautiful."

"Thanks." I smiled and turned around.

"Look at this," K.C said as he pulled out a tiny red velvet box.

"Oh hell no, you moving too fast." I shook my head.

"Nah, don't get your head too hype." He opened the box, and I noticed how small it was. It was a toe ring.

"Well I'm embarrassed." I smiled and grabbed the box.

"Nah, it's cool. You gonna be wanting to marry a nigga soon, so it's all good." He started doing the Dougie.

"Yeah, yeah." I had on open toed shoes, so I slipped it on. I had a surprise for him myself as thanks for how nice he'd been.

I grabbed the chain with his initials on it out of my purse. He covered his mouth and waved at his eyes like he was about to cry. I busted out laughing at his silly ass.

"Shawty got a nigga a present and shit," he said as he opened it and nodded his head in approval. "Shit is dope ma. I'ma wear it every game," he told me as he put it on.

"I love you, girl." K.C. pulled me into a kiss.

I was scared to say it back, but I was more scared that I might mean it.

****

The beginning of the party was as to be expected, with a lot of old people slowly circulating and gumming cupcakes and stuff. Their younger cousins started to show up, and that's when the party really started. I got excited when I saw Charmaine. Then K.C. and Anderson's mother showed up, and she gave me a big hug. That must have made that Ellie child upset because she was kissing her ass all night after that. Charmaine pulled me away from K.C to the bathroom of the hall.

"Who is that bitch with my cousin?" she asked as she put on lipstick in the mirror.

"I just met her when we flew off. She's kind of weird, ain't she?"

I replied.

"Bitch, she more than kinda. I don't like her. So, did you and my cousin become official?" She was still all in the mirror.

"Nah, but I think I'm falling for him."

"Aaaaaaaawww," she said with a smile. "He a good dude sis, I'm telling you. He might be whorish, but he had a good heart, and he won't cheat on you. Now that Anderson, he is a piece of fuckin' work, girl."

"I can imagine." I didn't say shit else as I put on more lipstick.

While we were chatting, Ellie walked in and she fake waved. Charmaine rolled her eyes and we walked out the bathroom. I saw K.C. dancing with some girl. so I decided to go sit down with Charmaine.

"Did you meet my uncle? That's K.C.'s father." She pointed at the older man sitting with their mom.

"Not yet." I shrugged at her.

"Come on." She walked me over to them, and I put on my largest smile.

"Uncle Monty, this K.C.'s boo thang." Charmaine smiled.

"Holy shit, look at this one." He got up and kissed my hand. "Bonnie, our boys got fine taste, just like their father." He looked over at their mom.

"Thanks, it's nice to meet you."

We sat and talked about my family life, and he seemed impressed that I had my own money and shit. When K.C. walked back over with the girl, I started to feel jealous, but I didn't let it show.

"Who is this?" The chick rolled her eyes.

"Stop acting stupid. This my shawty, Tori."

"Oh." She sat down on the other side of Monty."

"This is our ignorant ass daughter, Lexi." Bonnie shook her head.

"Well, tonight is the real party. I hope K.C got you a nice gown for the ball. My mother never went to her prom, so we gonna throw her something like it." Monty switched subjects.

"Well, he didn't, but I'm sure I can whip something up." I made a sweeping gesture with my hand.

"Tori, what do you do for a living?" Ellie asked out of no-where.

"I don't work yet, I'm just getting over an accident," I said and squinted.

"Oh, so I guess you're hitting the jackpot with Kadeem, huh?"

Everybody looked at her then me.

"First of all, if I never want to work in my life, I can do that. Jackpot? Let him tell it, I'm the catch, bitch. I don't know where your lil' jealous shit is coming from, but don't ever come for me again. You've sick since you saw me, and I promise you wanna get like me when you grow up." I snapped and every damn thing.

"Have you lost your mind?" Anderson said, grabbing her arm and pulling her to the stairs.

"I knew I didn't like that bitch," Charmaine said.

K.C. grabbed my hand, kissed his mother, and we headed to the stairs, that was the only way to exit. As we headed, out I could hear crying coming from the bottom.

"Let me grab the car," K.C. said and kissed me on the forehead before running out.

My interest was piqued, so I went down the stairs quietly until I made it to where the crying was coming from.

"Please spit on it at least," Ellie cried out.

"No, I want you to learn how I treat a stupid bitch, so you won't ever wanna be one again." He grunted. I could see him behind her, bent over.

"It's burning, baby," she cried out.

I realized he was stuffing her in the ass. I heard a car pull up by the door, and I ran back up. When I made it outside, K.C. was opening the door for me to hop in.

"OH MY GOD! KADEEM COATES!" A few teenage boys ran over.

"Can we get your autograph? Man, you just got signed to the Hawks, right?" the smallest one asked.

I smiled as he signed for all of those little boys. He winked and smiled at me the whole time. I leaned back and admired him living his dream; he was an inspiration to me.

"You ready?" He got in after the little guys left.

"That's has to feel good," I said, looking over to him.

"It does, that's why I got to go hard, ma. I love ball."

"I can see that. So, who is that bitch, Ellie, and why you think she attacking me like that? You think your brother told her about me?" I asked him.

"Who knows? Anderson is more mature than that, though. He wouldn't do nothing petty like that. I mean, he told me only because he called himself looking out for me." He shook his head and put the car into drive, then pulled off.

"Looking out, huh?"

I didn't get it. Was I not a human fucking being? Since I had an odd career choice, I don't deserve love? What kind of shit was that?

We spent the rest of the day laid out on the beach, waiting for the ball. He explained that the ball wasn't shit like what I thought it would be. Everybody will be dressed like hoes, and the men dressed like pimps. He said that's where his family came from. Weirdest shit I ever heard, but okay. I loved our time on the beach. He told me we could go jet skiing tomorrow. I was extra pressed to get through the night now.

****

"Are you sure this looks good?" I asked, pulling down the tight fitting dress.

"I'm sure. Damn girl, trust me."

I didn't feel comfortable with what I was wearing. I had on a spandex dress with a hole cut out the stomach. I had to admit I looked like a dime, but I felt like I was about to go turn a damn trick.

"Whatever. Everybody better be dressed like this." I punched his arm.

"They will. We did this for my mother too." He looked fine as hell in his red old school suit with the hat to match.

"We boutta crush shit," he said and pulled me to him.

"Yes, let's do it." I clapped and grabbed the shots I poured and threw mine back.

"Gimme mine, boo." He was fixing his tie in the mirror.

I handed him his and he threw his back as well.

"Okay so we gonna do this and have fun, then I'm taking you somewhere, aight? Just say yes." He swept my hair over my shoulder.

I pursed my lips and nodded.

Thirty minutes later, we were walked into a purple and black decorated ballroom full of skimpily dressed women everywhere. I was at a loss for words when their grandma and Bonnie walked up with less clothes than anybody. I didn't know if I wanted to throw up in my mouth or wait until I got to a bathroom.

"My new granddaughter showing off." She was shaking, and her sagging breasts seemed to move in slow motion.

"Thanks, and look at you." I raised my arms and hugged them both.

"Aight, come on, now. Your brother already in here showing you up on the dance floor, Kadeem," Bonnie said, pointing at Anderson and Ellie doing the Cha Cha slide.

"Oh hell nah. Come on, boo." He pulled me onto the floor and we started doing the dance with everybody else.

"Alright, it's couples only time. We about to play some old school jams," the DJ said.

The first song they put on was, "Always and Forever."

K.C and I pressed against each other and danced slowly. He smelled so good, and when I laid on his chest, I could hear his heart beating. I stopped listening to the music as I melted into his strong embrace.

"I like you a lot, Tori." He was almost reading my mind.

"I like you too." I smiled up at him. We sounded like kids.

"Just waiting on you, girl, then I can leave these hoes alone." He started laughing.

"I guess that's what I'm scared of. The type women who I'm going to have to compete against is gonna be fierce." I pouted.

"Ain't no competition. They put all that make up and shit on to look like you do without the shit. I ain't tripping off them fake hoes, they good for a fuck, but nothing else."

"I hope you keeping it 100. I think you need to enjoy the hoe years of the NBA. It's a lot of box out there."

"Yeah, but it's only once box I'm worried about at this exact moment." He went under my skirt and I hurriedly pushed it back down.

"Stop." I smacked his hand.

"Come to the car. I need that shit," he said and adjusted his dick.

"You not about to have me smelling like sex and shit. No sir," I said, fixing my skirt. "I got to go to the bathroom." I kissed him and walked off.

On my way, I saw Charmaine talking to some light bright dude in a pink suit. They really went all out for this.

When I got into the bathroom I ran to wipe myself. K.C. had me so wet I needed to clean up.

I heard a vibrating noise, and I remembered I put my phone on that setting. I grabbed it out my purse and I saw it was a North Carolina number. I scrunched my face and answered.

"Hello," I answered more like a question.

"Baby." I heard Donathon say on the other side. I sat quietly, not knowing what I should say to him.

"Hey," was all I could get out.

"I know you're surprised to hear from me. I'm in trouble," he said.

"Oh, now you want something to do with me when you need help. You selfish son of a bitch. So, when did you start robbing banks?" I screamed.

"Tori, please calm down. I know I have a lot of explaining to do.

"You damn right you do. But you can tell it to somebody else, I'm done." I was ready to hang up, he had some fucking nerve.

"Can we meet up?" he sounded so desperate.

"I'm in Miami with K.C.," I said without an explanation to keep him wondering.

The line was silent for at least 45 seconds.

"It's all good, Tori. You right, I shouldn't have called bothering you when I was the one who left you. I love you."

He hung up and I broke down in tears. I must have really been trying to fool myself thinking I had no emotions for him. I sent him a text.

I don't owe you shit, but when I get back I will call you.

I didn't check for a response, I just went back out to the party and enjoyed myself. Charmaine, of course, had me cracking up all night. She joaned on just about everybody in there. I definitely could get use to her, but Lexi was a different story. She was young, with a stupid ass attitude. I didn't know if it was because she was 18 and finding her own way, or if she was just trouble, but either way I was steering clear of her drama.

K.C spinned me in a circle and dipped me. I was holding on like he would drop me.

"Anderson wanted to know if you wanted to hit the strip club tonight. We were gonna do it last night, but he got into a little discrepancy with Ellie. I didn't tell K.C what I saw at the bottom of the stairs, but it never left my mind.

"That's fine." I needed a distraction from Donathon disturbing my new reality.

"Aight. We out in five minutes." He cupped my face and walked off.

I went and I said my good byes to everybody, and waited for K.C outside.

"Hey, Tori."

I jumped when I heard Anderson.

"You scared me," I said, holding my chest.

"Are you serious about this shit with K.C.?" His eyes were blood shot red. He was very drunk by the look and smell of him.

"You're drunk, go find Ellie and get her to drive you to where y'all staying." I turned to see what was taking K.C., so long when Anderson pulled me by my hair and kissed me.

I slapped him and pushed him back. "What the fuck are you doing?" I yelled at him.

"Oh, come on, Tori. Don't tell me you don't miss me. I know I was one of your favorites." He smiled and tried to come at me again.

"Look, even if I did enjoy it, we only crossed paths because of business," I explained to him.

"Well, let's make it old times. Nobody cums as beautiful as you do." He tried to kiss me again, but I ran up the steps and hit K.C's chest like a wall.

"Boo, you good?" he asked, making me look at him.

"Yeah, I was just coming to look for you." I sniffled.

"Oh, well you found me," he said, looking at Anderson like he knew something wasn't right.

"Pops looking for you," he said as he walked past him.

Son of a bitch.

***

The next few days, I decided to just spend my time with K.C. while we were in Miami. I refused to go anywhere with Anderson and Ellie. K.C. kept his promises and showed me Miami, and he won a lot of points with me. We went jet skiing, we had dinner on a yacht, and he took me shopping every day. There were so many females running up and smiling in his face, we had to leave one mall and go to another. I hated that we were about to fly back, but I guess reality needed to set back in.

"We can come back. The next time, we can do more," he said while helping me strap in on the air plane.

I didn't know what happened, but we flew by private jet alone. He didn't say shit about Anderson, so I guess those two decided to stay.

"Our first game is coming up, and I wanted you to be in the wife section," K.C said.

"I couldn't imagine sitting up with those basketball wives. I wouldn't blend," I nervously laughed.

"Yeah, you will. One day you gonna have a ring fatter than all them hoes." He kissed me.

"I hear you talking." I rolled my eyes and looked out the window.

"We gonna get it right. I'm letting you breathe right now, but when I'm ready, girl. You're gonna be a Coates." He grabbed my hand, looked at my ring finger, and nodded.

I knew he was just making his moves, but his game was cute.

We drank Champagne for the duration of the flight. He talked to me about his childhood and everything; he was really letting me in. I felt like I knew him so much better now. He said he had one more thing about himself that I didn't know, but he would reveal it to me when he was ready.

I was tired as hell by the time we pulled up in front of my house. He turned the car off, and we sat there for a minute in silence.

"What did my brother do after the party." He looked dead ahead.

Why is he asked me this now? I wondered.

"He was drunk. He said some stuff, that's all. No big deal." I wasn't one to be full of drama, so I wanted to make it nothing.

"You lying, Tori. He told me already. He said he was drunk, and tried to fuck, but you wasn't having it."

I squinted my eyes, if he knew, why the fuck was he asking?

"Well, now you know," I said then got out the car and walked toward my door.

"Girl, get your ass over here!" He walked up behind me.

"What? You act like it was a setup and shit. You wanted to see what I would do, huh?" I asked as I worked on my lock.

"No, I wanna know why you didn't tell me. I told you I ain't letting nobody fuck with you. so let me know when I need to check mufuckas." He snatched my keys and slowly put the key in and turned the lock.

"Thank you," I said and went inside.

"I guess I'm going now."

He caught my hand and slid me back over to him. The kiss he gave me let me know he was loving on me something serious. All the hurt I was going through had blocked my ability to reciprocate at one point, but that shit was out the window now. I was loving on his fine ass too.

"What you about to do?" he asked with his lips brushing mine with every word.

"You."

I kicked the door closed and took him upstairs to let him know how I felt with my body. While he slept it off, I went to try and call my mother again. She had yet to reach out since the day I left K.C.'s house. I was surprised to see 13 calls and 8 texts. They were all from Donathon.

I looked behind me to see if K.C was still asleep, then ran downstairs to go out back. I hit the call button and he answered right away.

"Tori, I need your help, baby," he said, breathing heavily.

"Well, what's wrong? Are you running or something?"

"Yeah, I'm running from the police station."

I didn't respond. I didn't know what to say. What the fuck?

Donathon

I didn't know what the fuck I was going to do, but I wasn't doing no fucking 89 years for shit. That's what they told me I could get for this shit. When I called that bitch Ellie to ask about my case, she told me everything was good. Come to find out, everything they needed to nail my ass came back, and I was wanted. I was stupid to go back to my house, but I didn't know where else to go, and since all my shit except my clothes was still there I was set. When they cuffed me and pulled into the station, I faked chest pains. They uncuffed me, and I took off running like Michael Johnson. I couldn't give my life to these motherfuckers.

I was happier than hell that Tori agreed to meet me at the convenience store down the street from her house. I sat with my head down under a hat I had just bought from the store. I heard a car horn blow three times just like we agreed. I ran over to Tori's Blue and white Audi. I opened the door and jumped in, all while looking around to make sure nobody was watching us.

"Don, what's going on?" she asked, looking confused.

"I just need you to trust me and drive." I looked at her, pleading with my eyes.

"Okay." She pulled off, and I told her to get onto the highway.

"I fucked up, baby," I told her with my hands over my face. "They wanna give me eighty-nine years." I let out an exhausted breath.

"They came and asked me about you, is that what all this is? How the fuck could you judge me, but you're doing this type of shit? And killing people, apparently." She was fighting back tears.

"I'm sorry, about everything."

"Oh, well that fixes shit. Donathon's sorry, everybody. Let's throw a fuckin' parade." The tears were now falling.

I grabbed her hand and she yanked it back. "Look, what do you want from me, so I can move on with my life?" she asked, looking over at me.

Even with red eyes and a snotty nose, she was beautiful.

"Let's leave. You have the house in Jamaica, and I have enough money in the offshore accounts. We can start over."

"Are you crazy? I'm not going anywhere with you. Just because I love you, I will let you stay there if you want. But as for me and you, I can't take any more of you walking away from me."

"So, you don't get how I felt or something? Imagine the roles switched, Tori. How the fuck did you want me to take that type of shit?"

"I already said I was sorry. I tried to kill myself, Don. Don't you see how fucked up I felt? You walked away when I needed you the most." She was trying to open the glove box, so I did it for her.

When she sat up, I saw she had a hickie on her neck.

"So, that's what it is? You got somebody else. It's K.C., ain't it?" I shook my head.

"See, that's how selfish you are. So what? What the fuck did you care who picked up the pieces after you broke my heart? We aren't together, but yes, I'm fucking him if that's what you were really asking. I also might love him if that's another question."

"That's cool," I said and leaned back.

"Oh hell no." She pulled off at the next exit and parked in a neighborhood about a block or so up.

"You son of a bitch! You wanted me to wait for you to be grown and deal with me? No! I am not your pick up and put down play thing, Don. You knew how much I loved you, you fucking knew it, and you still walked away. The only reason you come back is not to say baby take me back, but it's to ask me for help cleaning up your shit." She poked my chest. "So yes, another man came in and easily took your place. You didn't want the position, right?" she said with her nostrils flared.

She was pissed. The rain started as soon as I was about to ask her something I didn't really want to know.

"Do you love him?"

I looked into her eyes and got my answer. He took her heart from me.

"I do, and when I'm ready, I'm going to let him know just that."

Tori folded her lip into her mouth; she was about to break.

"Then be with him, baby. Don't worry about me."

I opened the door and got out. I started to walk off when I heard another door close. I turned around, and Tori was walking up to me. She slapped me so hard, I almost fell back. I looked at her like she was crazy, then I pushed her against a parked car and invaded her mouth with my tongue. She was kissing me back too. I knew she still loved me.

"I love you so much, girl," I whispered in her ear as the rain washed over us, making it a lot sexier.

"I love you too. I don't know what to do," she cried.

I had to keep kissing on her because I didn't know how long we had together.

"Are you coming?" I asked, hoping she would say yes, so we could forget about all of this shit here.

Her phone rang and she looked at me before answering.

"Hey. I got to call you right back, okay. Oh shut up, I miss you too." She stopped and smiled, and even blushed for a minute before hanging up.

"That's him. Damn, look how you smiling and shit."

She looked down at the ground.

"Come here." I took off my shirt, put it over her head, and walked her back to the car.

"I ain't tryin' to fuck you up no more than I did. I think I'ma try this shit on my own. I'm sorry for calling you with this shit." I kissed her soft, pretty ass lips and attempted to walk off.

"Don!"

I turned around and she waved me back over.

"Get in this damn car. I might can't stand you right now, but I'll be damned if you out here alone."

"Thank you," I said with relief.

After we got in the car, we realized that me taking flight probably wasn't going to happen since my name was all over the radio.

"You can stay in my pool house until I can get a way to get your ass to Jamaica."

"Ain't your boo gonna see me there?" I asked with too much jealousy.

"No, he won't. You're gonna stay your ass in the pool house until we can figure shit out."

"Tori—"

"Don't you mean Whori?" she shot back.

"I thought we just settled all that. I was hurt, so I tried to hurt you. Can we end that shit? Because honestly, my ass in some real deep shit, and I need you to still love me right now." I was begging her at this point.

We continued to drive in silence until we got to her house.

"Oh shit, get down," she said as she quickly hit the garage button and drove in.

"We should have drove past," I said, wondering why we didn't keep driving.

"They can't come into my house without a warrant, and since you're not known to live here, and we aren't married, they have no cause. So, calm down," she said, sounding all official and shit.

I could hear her door bell ringing, and she told me to go to her wine cellar, then go into the panic room and lock the door. I did what she said, and waited a while until I looked on the camera in the room and saw her slamming the door in their face. I breathed a little easier. I hit the open button and she came running up.

"They said an officer got hit while trying to chase you. They want you for his murder too."

"FUCK!"

3 Weeks Later

"They watching everything," I told Donathon as he paced back and forth through the living room in the pool house.

I can't believe this was us now. I was so in love with this boy, I lost him and got him back. only to lose him again. We just weren't meant to be, and we both had to accept that. I could lie and say being around his sexy ass didn't make me do flips in my drawers, but I couldn't imagine going there with him. I mean, K.C. and I weren't a couple, and I knew for a fact that he fucked other bitches, so what would he say to me?

"I don't know what to do." He sat back and kicked his leg out like an angry teen.

"Shit, I got a boat, remember?" I snapped my finger.

"Baby, I don't know how to drive no damn boat." He laughed.

"I'm trying," I said, then got up and headed to the door.

"Where you going?" he asked, scooting to the end of the couch.

"Do you really wanna know?" I asked with my arms folded.

"Well, you could keep it down. You know I can hear that shit, right?" He looked to the floor then back up at me.

"I don't mean for you to, but this is my house, Don."

It was something about how he looked at me that made my stomach knot up. K.C. had no idea he was in here when he came over. I was so scared he would see him one day walking around.

"I'm just going to the store, I was just teasing. So, your ears are safe tonight."

"Can I have you one last time?" he asked, pushing off the couch and quickly cornering me between him and the door.

This was the first time in three weeks that he tried it.

"You did, the night before graduation. Remember, you said you wanted to marry me, and the next day you asked. Then it was over a few hours later. So, you had me for the last time."

"Stop it. Tell me you don't want me to be inside you, Tori." He released his breath before touching my lips with his. I could feel my body tense up. I couldn't do this, I was trying to build something with K.C.

"I don't," I lied and opened the door.

"You do." He pulled me back in.

"Don, please."

I felt tears coming down my face because whatever feelings I had for him had rushed back at full speed.

"I just want to feel you." He kissed me, and I let him. "I love you so much, I won't stop loving you either." I walked with him to the bedroom and decided that it wasn't wrong.

"You have to go after this," I said.

"Why?" he asked.

"Because if you stay, I'm gonna fall back in love and wanna leave with you." I wiped my face of tears.

"Then I don't want to." He got up.

"Yes, you do." I pulled off my shorts and raised my arms up while he pulled my shirt up.

Donathon always had magic lips, so when he kissed my stomach, I felt the butterflies come. Soft kisses landed on every part of my body. He was about to go down, but I wanted him right now.

"Put it in," I whispered.

He pulled his pants down, pushed my legs back, and gave me what I been wanting since we kissed in the rain.

"I'ma miss you so much, girl."

"Me too, Don. Oh shit!" I wrapped my legs tightly and held on to him.

"Yeah, look at that face you makin', baby. Fuck, you got the best pussy I ever had." He was beating my spot up so good, I was pulling on him like a crazy bitch.

"I'm cumming!" I screamed out, and he started hitting the pussy harder.

"You gonna keep cumming, too." He flipped me over and stuffed his face into my pussy. I gripped the bed rails and felt my body jerk from his sucking on my clit. The fact that I just came had my clit sensitive.

"I can't take it, Don." I was ready to break down.

"Yes, you can."

He stopped and slowly slid his tongue in and out of my dripping wet pussy. My eyes started to cross after he latched back on to my clit. He abruptly stopped and grabbed my hair, pulling my head back to look at him. He parted my lips with his tongue and kept my mouth covered as he slid back inside of me. He was pinching my nipples, one at a time.

"You lucky I'm on birth control." I laughed.

"I wish you wasn't."

He got behind me and held me close. It wasn't that late in the afternoon, but I felt tired and we both lay there and went to sleep. When I woke up, Donathon was gone, and the only thing next to me was a note.

Baby,

Thank you, I cried when I woke up and realized I wouldn't be able to see you again. It's cool though, even though I don't like his dumb ass, K.C. got you, I know he do. I wish I didn't have to wash my dick, so I can keep your pussy on me forever, but that's nasty, so I guess I have our memories, right? I kissed you so many times before I left, but it still doesn't feel like enough. I put something for you under the pillow. I hope you don't mind, but I got the address for the house in Jamaica out of your office. I hope you come see me one day. I promise I will love your ass 'til I die, girl.

Wait, I wasn't done yet. I hope I did get you pregnant, though. Then you would have to come marry me and live in Jamaica forever. I love you again.

Don.

I lay back on the bed and rubbed the empty space. It really did feel good to make love to him one last time.

Bye, Don.

K.C

"The Hawks win it! Newcomer Kadeem Coates scored 28 points tonight, he came to play, and play, he did," the announcer blasted through the speakers.

I looked around for Tori, and I saw her coming down the steps to the floor.

"Good game, fool," Tori said, jumping into my arms and kissing me.

"You know it's because my lucky charm was sitting there looking bad as fuck." I humped on her with my tongue out.

"Boy, stop." She laughed.

"I got to go get changed. Do you wanna go back to the room, and I can get the hotel to make you feel like a celebrity?" I stole another kiss.

"Well, I am kind of tired. What y'all asses plan on doing?" she said with a smirk.

"Don't worry about that, boo. It's exactly what you think." I smiled and threw my towel at her. "Oh, and I got you a car waiting outside, too. See you later."

I trailed off down the hall. As soon as I got to my phone, I ordered her a massage and a big ass T-bone steak, a bake potato, and some cheese cake for dessert. The only whole bottle of good champagne was $1500, so I got her that and it would be delivered with strawberries. I was hoping by the time she cracked that and drank it, I could go put her ass to bed and eat them strawberries out her pussy.

"Aye Coates, I saw your lil shawty, man. That's bae, huh?" Antonio said. "Just make sure she ain't after the cash. We had to tell this nigga Gino about his baby mother man," Antonio continued.

"Shut the fuck up, like your wife got your best interest at heart, nigga," Gino shot back.

"Well, I ain't got to worry about that. My shorty got her own bread, house the size of mine, and pussy like red velvet cake, nigga." They all started laughing.

"Well, love on then, my nigga." Antonio fist pounded me.

We all got ourselves together, then hopped on the bus and rode off.

*****

"Oh yeah!" I hollered with the rest of my teammates as shawty popped her ass on the floor, making niggas go crazy.

We were celebrating our second victory at the Nasty Angels strip club. We had all the bitches in the club in our section, and we was making it rain something serious. Sirium was one of the only players I had gotten cool with, and he was the one who had set the ass fest up for us.

A few of them went to rooms and shit, but I decided to chill and watch while I waited for Tori to text me back. I wanted to make sure she got everything I ordered.

"Damn, daddy, look at you." This caramel bad bitch sat next to me, and she was looking like my type too.

"Who said you could sit down? Pop that pussy, ma."

I sat back and she got up and made her ass jump and clap while she was standing in place. After I threw some more money up, she got down, collecting and dancing at the same time. I finally heard my phone go off, and I saw it was Anderson's ass. I forgot I had invited that nigga out. He had been trying to grab some clientele from my teammates and shit. He had a meeting here in Ohio with some football nigga who play for the Browns.

"Wassup, bruh?" I tried to yell over the music.

"Where you at?" I could tell he was in the club because the music was the same.

"Come to VIP, nigga," I yelled and got up.

I could see him making his way through the crowd.

"Lil bro," he said, dapping me up and making a 'Damn' face at the broads.

"I ain't think you was coming, nigga." I leaned back and gave him the bottle of 1738.

"I need to ask you something. You remember ole boy Tori sidelined you for?" he asked.

I rolled my eyes because I know this nigga ain't come here to act like a bitch.

"Bruh, it's dead, just let—"

"Nigga, first of all, I was fucking drunk, aight. I wasn't trying to steal her from you, so shut the shit up. Look, she being watched, nigga. That dude got bodies and bank robberies, and he on the run. He gonna be calling her for help, and you need to make sure she don't get involved. Ellie is… was his lawyer, and the police came to her looking for him too."

I must have not been paying attention to shit because I hadn't heard nothing about it.

"Saw the news report, nigga, and she ain't stupid, man."

"Oh, she ain't? I ain't supposed to do this, but look." He pulled out his phone and pulled up a call log. I saw Tori's number a shit load of times. "They gonna lock her ass up if she helping him. Whatever she's doing needs to stop. You hear me?" he said, basically fucking up my whole night.

"I got it." I leaned back and took some more drinks down.

I couldn't have no type of fun after this nigga let me know I was looking stupid again. I didn't want to believe she would let this nigga get her into more shit after how he treated her ass.

"Yo, I'm boutta roll." I got up and dapped all them niggas up.

"Come on, Coates. The fuck? Nigga, its only one," Dean's big white ass yelled out.

"I got moves, man. See y'all niggas tomorrow."

I left out and realized I didn't have a fucking car, so I went into the private area and started checking the rooms for Anderson. I made it to the second to last and pulled the curtain back. I chuckled. He had two broads down on his dick, one sucking and one licking balls. I knocked and the two bitches jumped.

Anderson looked frustrated. "Damn, bro, it can't wait?"

"No, you fucked up my night, so I'm fucking up yours." I smirked.

"Man, fuck!" he got up and pushed the girls off him.

He was pissed the whole ride to the hotel, but I didn't give a fuck. I couldn't wait to get to Tori and ask about this shit. The valet walked up when we got to the front of the Hilton.

"Aight, bruh." I mushed his head and got out.

He sped off and put his middle finger out the window. I got on the elevator and put my card in for the penthouse suite. I was tapping my fingers in anticipation of making it up to the room.

The elevator dinged, letting me know I had gotten to the floor, and I bolted to the large door in front of me. I used my card to enter, and the smell of vanilla hit my nostrils immediately. I looked around and saw that the food was eaten and half the cheese cake.

"Tori!" I called out for her, but I didn't see her anywhere in this big ass suite.

As I got closer to the bathroom, the vanilla smell got stronger. I opened the door, and whatever I wanted to asked her about ain't mean shit at that moment. She was in a bubble bath, and her titties partially showed under the bubbles. The champagned was popped, and her eyes were closed while she butchered Mariah Carey's song. "We Belong Together."

I covered my ears and flashed the light to alert her of my presence. She looked up and gave me a huge smile. I sat in the tub next to her and got back to why I wanted to talk.

"Why didn't you tell me about your ex?" I didn't say too much because I wanted to see how she would react.

"I thought you knew." She picked up her glass and sipped.

"Don't talk to me like I'm stupid. You gonna get your ass bagged fucking with this nigga, shawty."

"I ain't fucking with him. He called and asked for help, okay?"

"And you know if you do help him, you're aiding, right? So, you think he worth throwing your life away for?" I asked.

"I didn't do anything, damn. Where am I? traveling with you like a groupie, that's where."

I still wasn't buying the shit.

"Did you fuck him?" I asked, ready to go the fuck off.

"Kadeem," she called me by my first name.

"DID YOU FUCK HIM!"

"Do you fuck all the girls calling your phone?"

"Tori, I promise I hate a fucking liar. Don't sit here and lie in my fuckin' face, girl. Know what. I think I deserve better than this shit." I got up and walked out the bathroom, and I could hear the water splashing.

"Stop." She ran up and grabbed my shirt.

"What, man! You still on bullshit and playing games with that fuck nigga, so go fuck with him, man. I'm trying to show you your worth, make you feel like I felt you should, and I think I finally realized one thing. One very clear thing. This ain't what you want, ma."

"It is! I love you, K.C. Please don't leave me," she said, breaking down. I looked at her trying to figure out if she was just saying anything to keep me there. "I swear, I told him I loved you the last time I saw him. I told him I would tell you when I was ready, and now is the perfect time. I love you, K.C., I said goodbye to him for good. Because I want to be with you." She licked her lips and pulled her bottom lip in.

"You sure about that?"

I walked out the room and went to the elevator. I felt so betrayed I didn't know what to do. I mean, yeah, I been getting pussy and shit, but I never lied about the shit, and I damn sure ain't putting my freedom in jeopardy over somebody who left me.

I could hear her crying loudly as I pushed the elevator. I looked at the door and exhaled deeply.

When I opened the door, she was in the fetal position crying her lungs out on the floor. I grabbed her off the floor and laid her down in the bed.

"Why are you back?" She wiped her eyes.

"I don't know," I said, telling the truth.

I don't why I walked back in this room, knowing she's been lying and shit to me. She still loved him more than anything, and it wasn't shit I was gonna do to change her mind.

"I don't want to be another person leaving you in your life, but look how you do this shit to yourself. You could have told me, Tori. I wouldn't have liked the shit, but if you wanted to stay with that nigga, you could have done just that. I didn't force shit on you, ma."

"K.C., I love you, I want to be with you. There is no more Donathon. Just Tori and Kadeem." Her eyes were blood shot red. But through all of that, I could see the sincerity.

"So, what you saying? You ready to be my girl now?"

"I'm ready to be whatever you want me to be." She came up and kissed me, and I kissed her back.

"Don't ever fuckin' lie to me again, Tori." I got up and flipped her over, and open palm smacked her ass four times.

"I won't." She cried and held on the sheets.

I kissed the red marks I left, and I could hear her moaning.

"Come on, so you can finish your bath." I pulled her off the bed and took her into the bathroom.

I was so mad at her, I took it out on her pussy. I wouldn't even let her ass sleep until I didn't have no more strokes left in my body. I went to bed still fucked up about her not saying shit. Yeah, I know she grown and could do what she wanted, but it was the fact that she held something from me, and I never lied to her. It's cool, better not happen again. I play games with nobody, and I didn't give a fuck who it was.

Rita

I called Donathons phone over and over trying to find out where the hell he was. I had fucked up so bad that I was taken off his case. Right now, I was going to a meeting with Anderson, and I hoped he didn't want to fuck because I was on my period and didn't feel like anal. I stopped to look into a mirror that hung over top of a table that held flowers.

"You better hurry up, he doesn't seem too happy," Rhonda, his personal assistant said.

I felt sick because I didn't know what the hell happened. I knocked and the door opened like he was waiting.

"Ms. Santia?" A large balding man asked. He had some little Lilliputian with him. Who the hell would fear him as a cop?

"Yes," I said with my heart almost beating out my chest.

"We need to know your last contact with Donathon Gray." I felt a sigh of relief. Anderson didn't looked relieved at all, though. He looked like he was about to fuck me up.

"I tried calling him a few times, but he isn't answering."

"Well are gonna need your information, and we'll keep in touch. If he calls you, let us know." He took out his pad, and I started to give them my number and address.

"Oh, we usually do a background on everybody who came in

contact with him, you know just to cover the bases. You don't have any prior relationship with the fugitive, do you?" the short one asked.

"No, I saw his case on TV and asked Mr Coates if we could take the case since it was high profile."

"Oh okay, so you wouldn't mind if we did our own looking, right?"

"No, not at all." I tried to sound as confident as possible, but I was scared shitless.

"Okay, good. We'll be in touch." They both walked out the door. I turned around to see Anderson sitting there with a smile on his face.

"You're a good liar, girl." He clapped his hands and even stood up and gave a standing ovation.

"What? I told them the truth."

"No, no, you didn't, Rita." He leaned back in his chair and folded his arms.

I started to laugh uncontrollably. "You fuck so many bitches in here you can't remember my name?" I asked, playing it off.

He threw a folder on the desk and I grabbed it and opened it.

"You were stupid to think your prints would come back as a different person." He shook his head.

"You know what, if this is your way of breaking shit off, then gladly." I walked backward and opened the door.

"Bitch, if you don't close that door, I will break your neck in two. Close it." I did what he said, and he got up and walked over to me.

He slapped me so hard across my face I fell against the door.

"I took you around my family, I gave you a job, I treated you like more than a murdering whore who sucks stranger's dick to get a gig. What the fuck was this for?" He asked, waiting for me to respond. "No answer, huh? Well, I see you're married to Donathon. So, of course, you knew who the fuck Tori was when you saw her. This is all about them, ain't it? You're so fucking pathetic, Rita. My brother is in love with that girl, and she is just as in love with him. She isn't worried about your fuck boy, and yet you're doing all of this to get back in with him. That's why you asked for the case. I should call the police right now," he said, picking up the phone.

"No, please. I have a son."

Anderson slammed his phone down. "What? You didn't say y —" He stopped and shook his head. "You took her baby, didn't you?" He looked completely disgusted.

"I have money, I can pay you whatever you want." I was desperate at this point.

"You're standing in my fucking building. Your money can't do shit for me."

"Then what do you want? If you wanted to turn me in, you would have."

"Nothing, you're fired," he said, waving his hand.

"Huh, you're not gonna tell?"

"You want me to?" he asked, shaking his head.

"No, thank you, thank you so much." I turned to run my ass out of there.

"Don't thank me yet. I need a favor," he said casually.

I exhaled deeply because he was irritating me, and he won't like me when I'm irritated or mad.

"What?" I rolled my eyes.

"Find him, I can get a lot of business for capturing a cop killer."

"I can't do that. He's my husband."

"He wasn't thinking about you when he was fucking Tori three ways from Sunday, so stop being a fucking punk and do what I told you. Oh, and if you think about running you won't get far. Somebody's always watching. Now get the fuck outta my sight." He looked down at his papers, and I walked out feeling like I had to kill his ass.

He thought he had me, but I was certified insane, and he had just got on my bad side.

*****

I didn't know the first clue on how I was supposed to find Donathon. The only thing I knew for sure was that I was going to pull Anderson's dick off with my hand and stuff it into his mouth.

"Shhhhhhhh."

I was putting my baby to sleep, and I wanted to cry. I couldn't imagine not being with him anymore. He was mine, and I didn't give a fuck what anybody said. As soon as he dozed off, I laid him in his crib and left his room. Marlina was sitting on the couch waiting for me when I entered the living room.

"What the hell are you going to do, Rita?" she asked, just as scared as I was.

"It's Ellie, okay! Stop fucking calling me that."

"Well, it's not like it's your name either." She rolled her eyes.

She was right about that too. See, my real name was Amarita Sanchez. Yes, I really had a psychology degree and I was licensed, but I had to change my name to get away from my past. My father was a Columbian drug lord, and he snitched and turned after he was arrested, so they have been looking for all of us to get revenge. I had stopped even thinking about that shit until now.

"Look, I just need you to help me find Donathon."

"For what? Get over it, damn. He doesn't love you, Rita. He moved on, and I think you should too."

I don't know what came over me, but I grabbed the first thing I touched and hit her in the head with it.

"What are you doing? You bitch." She tried to get up, and I hit her with the statue again

"HE LOVES ME! HE LOVES ME, TORI YOU BITCH! HE LOVES ME!" I screamed as I smashed her head in.

When I stopped for a breath, I realized what I had done.

"No, no, no. Marline."

I knew that trying to wake her was useless because her face was smashed, and I could smell shit which means she released her bowels. I had killed her. Fuck. I looked around in a panic because I had nothing to do with her body. I pulled the table off the area rug and rolled her up. Then I made a bold move and called my cousin, Raul. He was surprised to hear from me, and even more surprised when he got there and saw I wasn't what he remembered.

When he saw Marlina rolled in the rug, he shook his head and called somebody. After his friend showed up, the cleaned it up and took her body out for me.

"You need anything?" he asked before he left.

"No, I'm good." I was about to close the door. "Wait. I need you to take care of somebody for me."

I opened the door for him to come back in. Anderson was gonna learn he fucked with the wrong bitch.

Tori

"**I** can't believe you, boy." I had forgotten all about my birthday, but I guess K.C had no intention of forgetting it at all. He threw me a party on his new yacht, and though I didn't know half the people there, I was happy at the turn out.

"I got another surprise for you," he said, putting his finger up like he was telling me to hold on.

I smiled as I waited for him to come back up on deck. My mother came behind him.

"Mom." I walked up and hugged her.

"I forgive you, baby. I know I did a lot of shit to you, and I been trying to make them up to you by taking care of you now." She cried into my arms.

"It doesn't matter, Ma. I love you, okay." I pulled back and looked at her. I kissed her on the cheek and she smiled and wiped her tears.

"Thanks for coming." I wiped my tears.

"Of course," She pushed my hair back.

"I'm so proud of you, baby. I know I never said it, but you're amazing, Tori." She hugged me again.

"I love you."

"I love you too. Marcus would be so proud of you." She started tearing up.

"Have you seen Buffy?" I asked.

"Yeah, she scoped up the next available rich man. Your fathers partner." She shook her head.

"She had the baby?" I asked.

"Yeah, and they are raising it as their own."

"Wow. Well, enough of her. Have fun, okay?" I kissed her and went to see what K.C. and his friends where talking about.

"Baby, look at this nigga. You a female, so tell him that shit ain't cool." K.C. pointed at his teammate who had a Snickers bar logo cut into his low-cut beard on the side of his face.

I just burst out laughing and tapped his shoulder. They all started laughing with me.

"Fuck y'all." He turned up his drink.

"Baby, I know it's your birthday, but can you grab that bottle of VSOP out the bag? I sat in the room downstairs?" K.C. asked.

I put my hands on my hips and turned my lip up. I walked off and went to grab it for him. When I got downstairs, I could hear somebody talking on the phone behind the door.

"You find him, bitch. I promise your ass going to jail." It sounded like Anderson. He continued. "What you think he would do if he found out you were his lawyer the whole time, huh Rita? That facial surgery won't mean shit. Find Donathon, Rita, before I find you. Oh I'm sorry, Ellie right?"

I covered my mouth and ran upstairs. I couldn't tell K.C what I just heard. I ran back down and Anderson was already coming out the room. He smiled and handed me a box with a pink bow wrapped around it. I put on a fake smile and took it.

"I'm sorry again, about that night. I'm glad to see my brother happy," he said and put his hands in his pockets.

"I'm glad he makes me happy."

I started feeling antsy, so I went into the room.

"You heard from your ex lately?" He tapped his fingers on his side.

"No," I said flatly and grabbed the bottle.

"Oh, okay. Well, happy birthday again, Tori."

He walked out, and I sat on the bed, wondering what I should do. I took out my phone and texted Donathon. I didn't know where he was, but I made sure he knew it was urgent. I put my phone into my bra, fixed my pink tutu, and walked out. I walked up and gave K.C. his bottle.

"You good?" he asked, looking concerned.

"Yeah, it's a party. Boy, stop worrying." I smiled.

"Let's shake some ass then." He opened the bottle and poured his friends' cups and turned to me.

"It's your b-day, shawty turn your head back," he said.

I leaned back and he poured the liquor down my throat. Everybody started screaming and clapping.

"TURN UP!" I yelled.

We danced to every song that came on. Some of the players' wives and girlfriends circled me, and I was showing the fuck out. Twerking and all.

"GO SHAWTY, GO SHAWTY!" all the girls screamed. I was having the time of my life.

"You looks so cute!" Arlaine yelled in my ear.

She and I had become good friends since the season started. She backed up on me and started grinding. My face was hurting from all the smiling I was doing.

"Aye, aye!" I heard the microphone.

K.C stood in front of me and they turned the music off.

"I love you, girl, and I'm about to do something I haven't done since sixth grade to show you how you make me feel."

I was getting nervous as hell. What the fuck was he about to do. The music came back on, and I heard one of my favorite Chris Brown songs, except it was the beat.

"Girl let me fuck you back." K.C. sang.

Everybody went crazy, but I was just stuck. Somebody set a chair behind me and pulled me into the seat. I looked up and saw Charmaine smiling. I didn't even know she was here. She kissed my cheek.

"I know it's laaaate, I know its laate, but baby I can't focus. Focus. I just few in I'm back in town and hoping that you noticed. Noticed. I just posted my landing, aww. I hope we got the same old understanding awwww. I know you got up pretty early, I bee around bout 3:30, you usually done round one so baby when I wake you up! Just let me rooooocccck." He held the phone to everybody and they all said.

"AND FUCK YOU BACK TO SLEEP GIRL."

My mouth was hung open. I didn't know he could sing. He finished the song and pulled me up to him.

"I love you, girl," he said as he pulled out a ring and got down on one knee.

"I know we only been dating, as you say, but I got a feeling you always been mine. I just had to wait a little bit. It don't have to be next month or even next year, but will you promise to marry me?

Please?" he asked as he took my hand and put on the diamond ring that damn near broke my finger.

I looked into his eyes, and I couldn't do shit but smile from my heart.

"You damn right." I jumped on him and he swung me around.

"You serious?" he asked, looking at me.

"It took me a while to realize it, but you're for me. I love you, boy." I saw a tear come from his eye, and I kissed it away.

"We definitely gotta turn this shit up now," he said, holding me in one arm and lifting the other into a fist.

"I gotta wife, y'all!" he yelled.

"AYYYYYYE, LET'S FUCK THESE BOTTLES UP!" I didn't even see how yelled it, but everybody agreed, and we turned up the whole night.

K.C. kept the words to the song and fucked me to sleep that night. We stayed on the yacht and fucked the whole night until my ass passed out.

****

When I woke up, K.C. was still knocked out as usual after our sessions. I picked up my phone, remembering about Donathon. He had called me, and I knew I had to hit him back to warn him. I ran to the top deck and hit call back.

"Tori, what's wrong?" he asked in a panic. "Happy birth day too, I was scared to hit you just in case."

"Fuck my birthday. Where are you?" I hurried.

"I'm still in Texas, I'm still trying to figure out how to get my ass out of here. I think I got some help, though."

"Okay, I am gonna call around to see if I can charter you a flight."

"Come on, Donathon." I heard a female voice. A familiar one.

"Who is that? Is that Ellie, Don?"

"Yeah, why?" he asked.

"That's Rita, Don. She had surgery, get out of there. She setting you up."

"Tori, you not making sense. Rita's gone, even the police looking for her," he said.

"Don don't say her name." I heard a noise telling me the call was disconnected.

"Don!" I screamed. I tried to call him back, but he didn't answer.

"Tori?" I heard K.C. say from behind me.

"Hey, you. Good morning." I came up and he kissed me.

"I was looking for you, thought you went to the bathroom." He came up and kissed me.

"You found me." I kissed him again.

"You look red, baby."

"I am red, remember?" I giggled.

"I guess, so you know I'm leaving tonight for another away game. You rollin'?"

"No, I think I'ma sit this one out."

I felt like shit, but Donathon was in trouble. You know what? Fuck this. The tears started flowing before I could get out what I was about to say.

"What's wrong, boo?" he asked, looking concerned.

"It's Donathon."

"Oh my God, are you still talkin' about this nigga? I just asked you to marry me, shawty, what the fuck?" He stomped off.

"No, it's not what you think. He in trouble, I heard Anderson talking to Rita—"

"Who the hell is Rita? What the fuck are you talking about?"

"Shut up and listen! Ellie is Rita, Donathon's ex-wife. She's wanted for murder. She did something to him. Anderson told her to find him. I'm sorry, but I called and warned him. You can be mad at me, but I'm not letting him die," I said, standing my ground.

He took his phone out his sweat pants and stared at me while he called whoever it was he was calling.

"Who is this?" he asked with a look of confusion on his face. "No, you gotta be confused," he said, shaking his head.

The person must have hung up because he put his phone back in his pocket.

"You telling me the truth, Tori?" he asked, walking up and looking me dead in the eyes.

"I swear."

"Some nigga said he found Anderson's car running, phone and everything in it, sitting on Peach Road. Something ain't right." He went downstairs and ran behind him.

"What we gonna do?"

"You gonna go your ass to my house and wait," he said, throwing me some clothes.

"No, I'm not. I'm coming with you." I threw on some jeans and a button up shirt.

"Man, whatever. I don't give a fuck about that nigga, Donathon, but that bitch better not touch my brother."

I grabbed my purse and he snatched me out the room, basically dragging me behind him.

"Did he say where they were?" he asked with a look of desperation.

"I don't know. He had a house, but I doubt if he went there because the police were looking for him."

"Do you know where she lives?" he asked after closing my door.

When he got in the car, I continued.

"Let me check something." He pulled out his phone and made another call.

"Ciara, I need you to do me a favor," he said into the phone. He waited a minute, and I saw his face turn up. "Look, shut the fuck up and do what I tell you to do. I don't give a fuck if I ain't serving you dick no more, but you gon' do what I tell your ass." He barked into the phone.

I looked over when he said that, and he gave me the 'I wish you would' face.

"What the bitch whole name?" he asked me.

"Rita Gray is all I know," I said.

"Okay, try Rita gray," he said into the phone.

I waited in anticipation.

"What are you having her do?" I asked.

"She run a real estate company, she can find out if she owns property they could be at," he said and pulled the phone away from his ear.

"Yeah, oh for real? Okay, gimme that one." He took out piece of paper and a pen from his console and wrote an address down. "Thank you," he said and hung up.

"Did she find it?"

"She found Rita Oresito. I don't know if that's it, but we could at least give it a try."

"Thank you, so much K.C." I smiled and grabbed his arm.

"I ain't doing this for you. No matter how stupid the nigga is, I still don't wanna see Anderson fucked up out here," he said starting his car and drove off.

"I need to stop at my house first," I said, looking at him.

"Why?"

"We gonna need some shit."

He turned off in the direction of my house, and we got there so fast, I don't remember the drive. When we got inside, I went straight to my panic room and opened the chest I had for emergencies. I pulled out the revolver, the shot gun, and a .22."

"What the fuck you doing with all this?" K.C. asked, looking surprised.

"Just in case." I threw him the shot gun.

"You think we gonna need this shit for a bitch?" he asked.

"The bitch in question is a looney bitch. You never know."

He smiled and shook his head.

"You full of surprises, ain't you?"

"Yup, let's get this bitch."

*****

We pulled into an upscale condominium community and pulled into the first open space we saw.

"Let me say something real quick. I still love him, K.C., that much is true. But, I love you too, I'm in love with you, I wanna marry you, and give you as many kids as your dick can spit out. I don't care what reason you're doing this with me but, I still appreciate it. This is gonna be the last day I see Donathon Gray, and I promise he won't be an issue again. I want my future to be with you, Kadeem."

It burned my heart to say that, but I was being honest. Donathon and I didn't have a future, not a real one. I loved him, and will always have that huge space he put in my heart, but it will have to be from afar.

He locked fingers with me and kissed my hand.

"It's about time you figured that out. I already knew that shit years ago, I just had to be patient. I love you, ma." We shared a sweet, sexy, heart stirring kiss, and I felt like my soul transferred with his at that moment.

Our hearts finally understood each other, and we were locked into our love now. I had a smile on my face of true bliss, at this critical, dangerous, scary moment, I found the love of my life. We would have to continue this later because we had something to do.

"Let's go, shawty."

He got out and tucked the revolver in his waist. I grabbed the bag that carried the shot gun, then I put the .22 in my bra. And we started walking. We looked for the building number, but saw we were a few buildings down.

"There it is." He pointed.

My heart was pounding so fast because I was scared we were at the right place, I could just feel it.

"T2." I read aloud off the paper.

"It's on the ground, so it probably got one of those patios like that one we passed walking here."

That would be a lot easier because if we knocked, she wouldn't open it. I listened to see if I could hear anything. I heard cartoons on and a baby cooing. We might not be at the right spot. We ran around the building and saw that it did have a patio with a glass door. The vertical blinds were closed, but I could see at a slant that there was a baby in a high chair watching TV. I looked in the corner and gasped.

"Anderson!" I whispered loudly.

"What?" K.C. looked and saw Anderson tied up on the floor out cold.

He pulled at the door violently until it yanked open. We went in and heard loud music in the back.

"What the fuck?" K.C. said, trying to shake Anderson awake. I went toward the bedroom where I heard the music coming from. When I cracked the door open, I wasn't prepared for what I saw.

"Oh yeah, it's just like old times, baby." Rita moaned as she rode Don.

She had him in a chair with his hands behind his back and his mouth gagged. He was trying to get loose. This bitch was crazy. I kicked the door in and shot one time, missing her, but it made her jump off him.

"You trifling bitch!" I yelled, shooting at her and grazing her shoulder.

"Tori, run!" I heard K.C. yell before I was knocked out cold.

Donathon

"**W**hat the fuck are you doing here, Jackson? And what you do to K.C.?" Tori asked.

I recognized him from the graduation. He was the guy Tori got pregnant by.

"Oh, he's fine, look." He kicked K.C. and he started waking up.

"Who the fuck are you, and why are you in my place?" Rita asked, standing straight up to him, ass naked.

Crazy bitch. She force fed me Viagra and jumped on me for the last hour. I couldn't believe what the fuck was going on right now. This shit felt like a nightmare, and my baby was stuck in the middle now. All this shit was my fault. If I would have just let her live her life and moved on. Now we had this nigga holding a fucking gun to her, and I was tied up and couldn't do shit to stop this shit.

"I'm here for Tori so shut the fuck up and put some clothes on." He pointed the gun at Rita then turned back to Tori. "Baby I never stopped loving you. I missed you so much that I left my wife and been tracking you so I can see how to get you back. I saw you on your birthday and you looked so pretty. I been hoping you would forgive me and give professor long dick a chance. Then I see you with these two fuckheads." He kicked K.C again.

"Are you fucking kidding me?" Tori got up and walked up to him then slapped fire out his ass. "You treated me like trash. Why the fuck would I ever get back with you? I got pregnant, and had to have an abortion alone. You must have lost your fucking mind." She was standing toe to toe with him.

"You really need to reconsider," he said and pointed the gun at me.

"No!" She pushed him and he fell back, then the gun went off.

I pulled at my hands and started to get them out of the knots. I looked around the room and saw Rita make a move. I got up, still tied to the chair and ran into her to stop her. The chair broke when we fell, and I was able to get my hands free. I picked up the leg of the chair and stood over top of the bitch that ain't been shit but a fucking problem in my life, and hit her over and over with the wooden leg. I stopped when I heard the baby crying in the other room. I saw that Tori and Jackson were gone. I buttoned my jeans and went to wake K.C. up.

"Aye." I shook him.

He was alert now and he started looking around for Tori. "That dude just grabbed her. We can catch 'em hurry up," I said, running out to see a nigga laid in the corner tied up. I had to make the stupidest move for the sake of the baby.

"Call the police and give them the address," I told K.C.

We both ran out and he called while we tried to catch up. I could hear Tori screaming for help further down the street. I started running faster until I saw him trying to push her into a car. She was whooping his ass too.

"Let her go!" I ran up, but he turned and pulled the gun again.

"I will kill this bitch before I let y'all have her," he said, putting the gun to Tori's head.

"Stop!" I screamed. "You gonna have to kill me then, bruh.

"Because she ain't going nowhere with you," I said and walked up.

He tried to shoot me, but the gun jammed. I took that chance to rush him. K.C. pulled Tori out the way. I started beating him into the ground. I took the gun and saw he had the safety on. Fucking idiot. I took the safety off, and put one right through his forehead.

"Don." Tori cried.

I didn't give a fuck if that nigga was holding her. I pulled her right out his arms and kissed her forehead.

"Nigga."

"I know, but you can't let me say bye to the only woman I ever loved?" I asked.

"You got one minute, my nigga." He looked with a grimace on his face.

"So, where you going?" Tori asked.

"I don't know, but I gotta go, they called the police. Go get that baby, and make sure they know what happened, okay?" I told her.

I wanted to kiss her so bad, but I didn't feel like fighting this nigga. She mouthed, *I love you* but me, I was grown.

"I love you, Tori Minors," I said aloud.

While holding her hand, I felt the ring she wore on her ring finger.

"You getting married?" I asked, feeling like my heart got ripped out.

I couldn't give her shit but a prison record, so all I could do was be happy that she could get more from him.

"Yeah, we are." She smiled and grabbed K.C.'s hand.

All I could do was think about when I proposed and how ready I was to make her my wife. I heard sirens and I knew I had to go.

"Take care of yourself, Don," she said as she walked off with K.C. toward the condo.

I saw the lights reflecting, and I started to run. Another unit came from the other side and stopped my progression.

"That's Donathon Gray!" one of the officers yelled out.

I saw them file out their car, and I thought about running, but where would I go?

"Don!" I heard Tori yell.

K.C. was holding her while she cried and tried to reach out for me. I felt like time moved in slow motion for a minute. I saw that I was in a hopeless situation.

"You got my heart, baby." I yelled to Tori and took off running.

The first shot went through my leg, but that didn't stop me. The second one hit me in the side, and the third in my back. I collapsed on the ground and tried to crawl, but my legs started to feel numb.

"Nooooo!" I heard Tori cry out. She appeared over me, and lifted my head off the ground.

"Don't go. I love you, Donathon," Tori cried over me.

"I have to. I have to go, so you can be happy. I love you, baby," I said before I started to see her fade out of my vision.

I Loved you til death baby, just like I promised.

Tori

2 years

"Push, baby. I can see the head." K.C. yelled in my ear, he was getting on my fucking nerves too.

"I know to push, dammit, so stop telling me to do something. I'm already doing!" I yelled at him.

"I don't know. I be seeing that shit on TV. I thought that's what I was supposed to say."

"I can see the head," the doctor called out.

I pushed hard two more times, and I heard our baby crying his little lungs out.

"Kadeem Jr., in this bitch!" K.C. screamed out.

I felt like my pussy had been ripped open, which it had.

"Here's your baby boy one, he laid the first twin in my arms. I pushed three more times, and our baby girl came out.

"Kanise just turnt the shit up," K.C. yelled again.

"Shut the hell up." I laughed.

I looked down at both of my babies and saw they looked just like K.C., chocolate drops. I smiled at my husband, and I could tell he had never been so proud. This and the day we got married. Two months after Donathon died, we threw a big ass wedding at the Falcon's dome. I haven't had a bad day since the day we said I do.

I missed Donathon so much, and it hurts my heart to flash back to the day he left for the last time, forever. He was still as handsome as the day I met him when he laid in his casket. I cried for days, and K.C. let me grieve without interruption. He was there for me. I loved him so much.

Rita didn't die when her head got bashed in. She is in a wheelchair because Donathon damaged her spine when he tackled her. She had two life sentences, thank God. The police gave the baby to the mother's family to raise.

My mother and I started all the way over. We talk every day, and she got herself off those pills and even got engaged to one of the lead Psychology professors in DC.

Jackson, that fucking lunatic did die, and his wife released his body to science and told them to see if they could find a man inside of him. I couldn't believe he was stalking me. It was so out of left field that I didn't know what to even think when I saw him standing in that doorway.

Unfortunately for Anderson, he survived enough to get locked up for aiding and abetting Rita aka Ellie. She recorded their phone calls and told the police where to find them. She told them he knew the whole time, and he would fly her on trips and even gave her a job, and he didn't have much of a defense since he did do those things. That's what he gets for trying to be a bastard.

To be honest, I was glad all this shit was over with. All the drama was a little too much to handle. I could move on in my life, and now I would never have to ask this man will he still love me tomorrow because I knew he would.

The end